OLGA BOGDAN

Helena

The Small Town Throwdown

ttt

Published by TruerThanTruth Production 2017
www.truerthantruth.com

© 2017 Olga Bogdan

Cover photograph by Alberto Monteraz
montechrome.format.com

Cover design by Tim Peplow

Interior design by Polgarus Studio
polgarusstudio.com

For all enquiries, please contact:
info@truerthantruth.com
info@olgabogdan.com

HELENA

ISBN 978-1-9998043-0-5 (paperback)
ISBN 978-1-9998043-1-2 (e-book)

With special thanks to Helen Baggott and Valentina Djordjević.

CONTENTS

HELENA

WELCOME TO MY NIGHTMARE

I come round into the slurry pit of somebody else's life. I know this is not my life, couldn't be, I'm not so stupid as to own such a thing. I also know my body's going to hurt, but then again my body always does that. Hurts. Kid you not. You point a finger at it and it's bruised. Anyway. Time to face the music.

I unpeel my eyelids. Where am I. Question mark. And when – it's dark in here, but I'm not exactly sure if this is dusk or dawn kind of darkness. Normally, this wouldn't bother me too much, but there are times when a girl could do with having a semblance of her so-called bearings. Like for example, right now.

So bloody dark. And smelly. Can't quite put my finger on it, wouldn't really want to; I mean, who'd want to touch a diseased toenail liberally dusted with lily of the valley-scented talcum powder. Because that's what it smells like around here. Seriously. I must get out of this place before I throw up all over my last night's finest. I check in with my fingers, knees, hips, shoulders and any other bits I can think of, which enables me to arrive at the following conclusion:

a) My body parts all appear present and more or

1

less unharmed, and spread across something hard, my guess would be the floor, and

b) I'm fully dressed. Thank God for small mercies, is all I'm saying.

I drag myself into a sitting position. My head explodes. 'Mother f–'

'Shhhhhh!'

Who dares hush me in my hour of need. Out of the shadows emerges a small child, maybe a boy, maybe a girl, maybe a demon. Dead black eyes; I bet this is what it feels to look down the barrel of a loaded .44 Remington Magnum.

'Um… Hi?'

The next thing I know, the creature's on top of me, its bony hands pressed over my mouth.

'Shhhhhh!' it goes. 'Shhhhhh!'

I push it away. This is all getting a bit too surreal, even for my liking. Time to bolt. But first, I take a moment to assess my current predicament:

a) I'm sitting on the floor in some kind of a kitchen. I say it's a kitchen because it has a camping gas stove in one corner, and an assortment of plastic plates, cutlery and tin cups in another; I can't guarantee it's a kitchen because the room also houses two cots, each occupied by a rather grubby looking human looking baby. Reckon they're sleeping, on account of not moving, but equally they could well be dead. In any case, I have just successfully located the source of that horrible stink, and where is my medal;

b) the creature in front of me is a boy. I can see his little willy wagging at me from underneath his moth-eaten purple cardigan. I feel embarrassed, I feel hot, I feel very, very bothered, and

c) somebody's having sex close by. I look around, there's a door behind me, offering an eerie glimpse into a darkened room. I hear a woman's voice, muffled, then a man's voice, raspy and cracked, and not in a good way. Another man's voice asks for matches, then still another man laughs a keen little laugh.

Cold sweat pours down my back. That's right, pours. And I never even sweat that much. How very disgusting of me. I get up and head for the door directly opposite the room my brain is busy comparing to the right panel of that Hieronymus Bosch triptych; great timing, brain, and where were you when I needed you the most. The creature-child crawls in between my feet. I motion it to move the fuck out of my way. It stares back at me, in what you might call a belligerent fashion. My heart is pumping hard now, my head is returning to a semblance of making sense. I grab the creature by its scrawny shoulders, force it off my path and push open the door. I'm just about to step out onto a sun-drenched pavement, when I feel a stinging pain in my left leg. I turn around, and see the creature has sunk its teeth into my calf, and basically gone feral on me, growling like a dog and everything. I could hear the voices rising from the back room.

'Get off!' I say. But the boy-thing doesn't seem to hear me, so I kick it, as gently as I dare, but still hard enough for it to let the fuck go and fall back into the darkness.

I limp off down the street, as fast as I can, feeling

the warm blood trickling down my leg. And just before I turn the corner, I hear a child cry, a woman scream, and a sound of a door slamming shut on the world I leave behind.

'Next to the children's dispensary?'
    'Yes. In the building right next to it.'
    'How much did you have to drink?'
    'How should I know – a lot?'
    I'm sitting on Iva's bed. She's helping me figure out what happened to me last night – yet another big night out in a small town gone horribly wrong. The story of my so-called life. Iva has cleaned and dressed the wound, made me rest my leg on a pile of soft velvet cushions. Nice. We are waiting for her mum to return from work and administer a tetanus shot. I'm not convinced this is entirely necessary, but Iva's mum is a doctor; guess I may as well do as she tells me. Plus, I'm so traumatised not to mention haunted by the visions of those vile babies sharing that squalid dark room with The Creature and God only knows what else, the more drugs the merrier as far as I'm concerned.
    'You kill me, Helena,' says Iva. 'What the fuck were you thinking, going around a junkie whore's den?'
    'First of all, I didn't go around of my own volition, I must've been kidnapped.' I light a cigarette. 'Secondly, don't bring it down, I may write a story about it one day. Thirdly, how do you know where I went? I don't even know where I went.'
    'You know I know everything.' This, by the way,

was true. Iva knew everything and everyone. She must've been cursed by a gypsy or something. 'The woman who lives next to the children's dispensary happens to be Dad's favourite proof that socialism doesn't work. Her name's Melita. She used to be just like us–'

'There's no-one else like us!' I say. 'How dare you?'

'Alright then: Melita was a proper Vukovar girl, plain and good, so definitely nothing like us. She used to work at the shoe factory, all the women on the factory floor thought she was too stuck up for her own good. But Dad said she was just a dreamer, a lost soul who preferred to stay lost.'

'I like being lost,' I say. 'As long as I know where I am.'

'Thank you for that valuable insight. But this is not about you, so please don't interrupt.'

I make a zipping movement across my lips.

Iva sits beside me, and lights a cigarette. 'Melita never took the factory bus, she preferred to walk to work, rain or shine.'

'Are you making this up?'

'Right!' Iva re-zips and locks my lips, and throws away the key. Although I do appreciate the key is highly imaginary, I catch my eyes search for it amongst the clothes lying on the floor where it was supposed to land. Stop it, eyes. 'One winter afternoon, as she strolled by the river on her way home, wrapped up in her thoughts as well as a thick woollen scarf and a rabbit hat that muffled all sound as well as sense of approaching danger, she got gang-raped by a bunch of the factory guys – and nine months later she gave birth to a beautiful baby boy.'

'Can we talk about something else now, my savaged leg for example,' I say. 'I had enough social realism for one day.'

'I'm not done yet,' says Iva. 'So there she is, lying in the hospital bed, the rape-baby by her side, and her mum walks in, tells her she's no longer welcome home. Brought shame on the family, and all that. Dad steps up, way above and beyond his police duty, persuades this doctor to let Melita and her baby stay at the hospital until the social services come up with a place for them to live. But other women on the ward, they don't want a whore amongst them, so they literally witch-hunt her out of the hospital, wearing only a dressing gown and with her baby suckling at her breast... So the poor girl finally loses her marbles, and it was only down to the intervention of the kind doctor, and Dad of course, that she was allowed to keep the boy.'

'That must be the creature who bit me. It's dangerous. I want it shot.'

'All heart, you are.'

'I know.' I try to think of another compassionate thing to say. 'And I hope they shot the men who raped her.'

'Are you kidding?' says Iva. 'No one saw anything, therefore no one did anything. Those guys bragged about their deed practically everywhere except at the Sunday Mass, but there were no witnesses, no evidence, nothing to connect any of them to what had happened to Melita. It drove Dad half-crazy. In the end, his boss ordered him to stop the investigation, and stop it dead. He told Dad, "As far as we know, it was consensual. A harmless bit of fun. We can't send those young men to prison for having a bit of a laugh, can you now?".'

Was that a proper question. Like, with a question mark. I sometimes have a difficulty telling. I don't do question marks any more, because I am no longer interested in finding out the so-called answers. But, judging by the look on Iva's face, I can tell she is. So I say, 'Not in this town you can't.'

'Exactly!' Iva seems pleased with my answer. 'Or this country. Dad was never the same after having to drop that case. He had lost all faith in the government and has been working on bringing it down ever since.'

Bringing what down? Is Iva talking politics again? Time for a subtle change of subject. 'Can I have a glass of wine?'

Iva stares at me. 'I really feel like slapping you right now.'

What? Perhaps I've overstayed my welcome. I feel a pang of self-pity. And rage. 'Do you want me to leave?'

She rolls her eyes. 'Christ. No. Of course I don't want you to leave.' She sighs. 'I'll get a bottle. Just don't go mad, okay, don't overdo it.'

'I won't,' I lie.

What's the point of drinking if you're not going to overdo it.

THE KINGDOM OF
PRINCE LAZAR OF SERBIA
Kosovo Plain
15th June 1389.

I look towards the east. A poet would perhaps be tempted to call the sun hesitant to inflict another day upon this blood-drenched corner of the world. But I am not a poet. I know it is not up to the sun to decide what it will shine upon and when. Despite its role as the centre of the solar system, its only job remains to glare ceaselessly on, detached from both its cause and its effect. It is not up to the sun to discern, let alone endorse or condemn yet another scar appearing on the surface of Earth as it rotates into the light. No matter what, the sun also rises. And, as the shadows of the night part to reveal the first glimpse of Kosovo Plain battlefield, I almost wish it would not.

Seventy-two hours of fighting has left the ground strewn with Christian and Ottoman flesh, spreading bloodlust amongst the great black ravens and dusky-grey crows. I watch as their sharp beaks pluck the flesh clear off the bone and tear away long strips off the fallen soldiers, both dead and alive, before dropping them on the ground and returning for more. No longer hungry, these birds act as if drunk on princely offerings of flesh and blood. Living alongside humans has certain consequences. The human condition has a remarkable tendency to spread like a wildfire that shows no mercy as it attempts to devour the rest of the world.

This is where I come in: my job here is to snuff out the life that has, for all intents and purposes, already expired. People call me many different things, most often an angel of mercy, or an angel of death. Some even call me the Death itself, the Almighty Reaper, the One Who Appropriates. I have been around for long, long years, yet I still find myself moved by people's insistence on death being their main and only ruler, the sole destination of their life's journey. The truth is, the journey's never over. Another truth? Human beings have great difficulties facing up to the truth. Talking of which, my human name is Baba Lepa – pretty granny. It was given to me within the first couple of years at the start of my Balkan assignment. I like it. Balkan people may have proven the most difficult to move on, but they show a good sense of humour, even at their deathbed.

The wind changes direction. As the smell of wounded flesh and curdled blood forces its way up my nostrils, I decide it is nigh time for this pretty granny to embark upon some not so pretty work.

I don't merely snuff the life out of a person, first I must bring grace to their last moments here on earth. Such is the law. No matter what they have done, how badly they have behaved, or what crimes they have committed during their lifetime – none of it matters one single iota when it comes to a person's dying hour. Grace must enter them before they can move on. This, of course, can be a tall order, as the vast majority of people feel powerfully disinclined to die. Even the worst of lives suddenly appear a rather more superior proposition to death, however graceful or glorious. I try to sweet-talk them into walking over the threshold willingly and without fear, but on its own this rarely works. Instead, they spit and snap at me, and – if they're physically able – they try their best to snuff me out first.

As grace cannot enter before the conditions of surrender and acceptance have been firmly established, I often resort to something called glimpsing. Considered by the puritans in my field as cheating, glimpsing is the way of showing a dying person the reality of their situation beyond their immediate predicament, which never fails to inspire them to let go of just enough fear for grace to slip in. And with that, they can be on their way. What is a little cheating, I say, compared to all the suffering the puritans subject their clients to? It can take days, months, even years for a person to be snuffed out without glimpsing. I avoid the puritans like the plague. Not that I need to avoid the plague: plague victims made for some of my best clients.

Summer battles are the worst. It is the heat, dissolving everything that remains into a putrid mush. At some point during the course of the morning, a little ditty starts running through my head, without ever passing my lips:

Life and death become one,
Mangled by the midday sun.

On and on it goes, round and round in my head. I have cleared only about a fifth of the field, but I know my job gets easier with every passing hour. Back on the ground, there are a couple of Turks sprawled to my left: one has been cut down across the chest, the other's head is attached to his neck by a thin strip of skin and sinew. They no longer require my services. Next to them, a young boy is lying on his back, his eyeless sockets staring at the sky, his fingers still clutching the blooded leather water flask. Christian boy, a water bearer. I look closer at the flask, just about distinguish a pair of bull's horns, a two-headed eagle and a dragon, all part of Prince Lazar's coat of arms. One more Serbian mother is to have her heart broken – one of many yet to come.

I am just about to step over a horse cadaver in order to make my way to a body swathed in ravens, when I hear voices. This is a highly unusual occurrence in the aftermath of any battle. The absence of sound comes with the territory, even birds feast in silence – no need to make a fuss in the land of plenty. An occasional moan, a flap of wings, a soft squelch of a boot as survivors return to the field to sift through their fallen comrades for any signs of life; no other sound is appropriate in the land of death. I shoo the ravens away. The man's face is missing, as well as most of his brain and his gut. He is long gone.

I listen up. The voices are coming from behind a large rock in front of me. They sound jaunty. Mirth in the middle of Kosovo Plain? That I must see.

Two men are sitting with their backs against the rock. One is dark-skinned, almost as dark as any Turk, but with curly auburn hair, high cheeks and bright blue eyes, indicating a possible mix of Celtic and Slavic provenance. When it comes to the Balkan folk, one can never be too sure who they really are, or where they come from, or which way they are heading. Their capacity to surprise is unparalleled by any other race I have dealt with in the past – they slip, they flip and in a blink of an eye they become something other than you first suspected them to be. I have been studying the peoples of the Balkans for over 9,000 years now, and can only conclude that their chronic inconsistency, their inclination to startle and confuse stems solely from their untameable nature, and not from any painstakingly developed manipulation design. The problem is, this chameleon-like behaviour can come across as a threat and a challenge, and has been known to provoke an aggression from other tribes in the past, as it will continue to do until the end of time – or until the Balkan folk learn how to tame their wildish ways. And I have a feeling I know which scenario is likely to occur first.

The other man is paler, with just enough salt and pepper hair poking out of his winged helmet to identify him as an elder.

'Well, my brother Ivan.' He knocks on his bashed-in breastplate. 'I hope you like roast pork, for I am almost done.'

'Take it off, brother Vuk,' says Ivan. 'I would offer to assist you, alas…'

'I thank you, my brother, but I fear only an armorer can assist me now.' Vuk starts to cough. A thin streak of blood trickles out of the corner of his mouth. He wipes it off with a back of his hand. 'Or a priest.'

'Forgive me, but that is the heat talking. The sun is rendering you feeble.' Ivan leans towards Vuk. 'Hear me out, my brother. People come to Vrane from far and wide, and they speak of the greatness of Serbian warriors and their magnificently courageous spirit. I am privileged to find this to be true. Once we get off this blessed plain, you will come and visit my castle perched high on the cliff at the edge of the lake. We will ride out together, side by side, back to my home in golden Croatia; we will spend our days hunting for wild beasts and our nights sitting on the terrace under the canopy of vines and stars, and we will drink red wine and eat baby lambs straight off the spit, and we will caress milky-skinned Croatian maidens. But most of all we will rejoice in our Slavic soul triumphing over the unclean.'

'And so it is: let it be so,' says Vuk. 'For you are no longer my brother by a distant father, you are now my brother in destiny. The people of Serbia will never forget the righteous Croatian knights who rushed to aid our noble Prince when he needed you the most. There will be songs performed in your honour, long after you and I are gone, and they will tell the story of the band of brave Croatian men, leaving their wives and their sons behind, forsaking their fields and their flotillas, and riding four days and four nights without rest in order to help the Serbian army keep the Ottoman dogs out of our backyard. You fought with me side by side, my brother, so it is only right to rejoice in the same vein. Together, we brought Murad down, may his god greet him at the gates of paradise as a king and a hero that he truly once was.' Both men cross themselves. I notice Ivan's right hand is missing. Vuk continues, 'It is my honour to finally meet one of the legendary Croat soldiers, to fight with him, shoulder to shoulder, and to fall with him, like a hero and a brother, victorious over Ottoman scum, God bless their warrior souls.'

'Exult, my brother Vuk,' says Ivan. 'For I see the help is here.' He motions towards me as if he has only just seen me, even though I have been standing right in front of him this entire time. 'You! Yes, you, old crone, stop wasting precious time, but come over and tend to my brother Vuk and his noble wounds!'

'I would be careful who I call an old crone if I were you, young knight,' I say. 'Considering how it is you who needs assistance from me, and not the other way around.'

Ivan curses. 'You would not be speaking to me like this if I still had my hand, old woman! For you would have no tongue to speak with!'

I stand there, and I smile. The fact that Ivan can see me indicates his readiness to move on. Except that he does not know this yet. I glance at his Serbian comrade. At first he looks at Ivan as if he were a madman, but then, slowly, he focuses on the space I inhabit until he can see me as clearly as only the dying could. And once he has seen me, his entire body relaxes, at which point grace enters him.

'Welcome, my lady,' he says. 'Welcome. And please forgive my friend, he is too young to have acquired respect for your kind.'

'What are you saying, my brother?' Ivan waves his remaining hand in my direction. 'She is but an old witch, here to rob the corpses! Go on, brother Vuk, you can still hold your weapon, make her help us!'

'I cannot speak for you,' says Vuk. 'But it is too late for me. I welcome this noble lady. She will help me pass through to the other side.'

I curtesy. 'Thank you, kind sir.'

'Wait! Wait, I say!' Ivan turns to me. 'Listen up, you old vulture, help us live, and I swear on my ancestors' bones you will be rewarded beyond your wildest dreams. But do anything to bring about our demise, and I will personally haunt you for the rest of eternity. Do you understand the choice that lies before you?'

'I do, young sir,' I say. 'The question is, do you understand the fact that you have no other choice but to heed the call?'

Ivan opens his mouth, then closes it again without uttering another word. He then looks down at the pool of blood he has been sitting in since the last sunset, and it is as if he is seeing it for the very first time. 'But,' he softly says. 'My bride, she awaits me.'

'You will meet Marica again,' I say. And again.

And again. This is not the biggest of worlds. 'But not in this life.'

Ivan's eyes widen. 'Really?' I nod. 'But how can I know for sure?'

I kneel between the two men and take their hands in mine. 'Because my words are true. As you leave this world, know that you are never really leaving behind anything or anybody you hold dear to your heart. Know that you can never lose love, you can only temporarily lose the sight of it, and this is true in death as it is in life.'

'Thank you,' says Vuk, and with that, he is gone.

I turn to Ivan, who is smiling at the apparition of a beautiful young woman running towards him, her arms open wide, her eyes filled with joy. And just as it reaches him, he, too, is gone.

I place my mark on their respective foreheads, which will protect their bodies from scavengers, then walk over to a young Turk who has been unfortunate enough to have a spear pierced right through his middle, nailing him fast to the ground. He looks up as I arrive, and, despite his faith promising that everything he longs for in this world will be awaiting him in Jannah, he still does not seem too pleased to see me.

SWEET SIXTEEN

The year's 1991. My name's Helena Ferlan. I'm a sixteen-year-old college student, doing my second year at the Vukovar Gymnasium, which is neither here or there because I have already chosen my path and it has nothing to do with any college curriculum. Still, I make sure I sail through my exams, get straight As, and all that crap. It's easy for me, not only because I'm super clever, but also focused. I want to get myself out of this black hole as soon as I can, and the university seems like a convenient stepping stone. Not that I plan to actually study anything those people have on offer, it's just the case of the better I do, the better my chance of getting into the university of my choice. Like Mum keeps telling me, annoying broken record that she is.

I want to go to Oxford, or La Sorbonne.

'Belgrade or maybe Zagreb,' says Dad. 'You won't find better education abroad.'

Bet it would be a very different story were I to express a sudden burning desire to study at the Moscow State University. I bet he'd see this ongoing studying abroad saga, as he likes to call it, in a brand new light. And I bet he'd move heaven and earth, resort to bribe and blackmail if he had to, and basically do everything in his power in order to secure his older, and may I add favourite, daughter a place on any course she bloody well chooses. Mother Russia, *über alles*.

Although, hand on heart, I'm not convinced he'd do any of the above. Dad really is as straight as they come. A man of integrity. And a natural-born communist, can you believe my luck. He even gets upset if people call him an intellectual, or god forbid – an academic.

'I'm just another worker bee,' he'd say. 'No different from anyone else.'

'Dad, you're a writer,' I point out. 'A historian. That makes you an academic. Give me a break.'

He smiles underneath his not very grown-up moustache, and repeats, 'Just another worker bee.' Or, cue a big cringe, 'I'm just another brick in the wall.' Then he turns back to his daily chess puzzle in Politika, which he studies over his lunch, typically something warm and soupy, like a bowl of bean and smoked sausage stew with a piece of a couple of days old bread. He prefers stale bread, says the fresh bread makes him constipated. As if we really need to know such a gory detail.

I know that in a few years' time I'm going to live in London, or maybe Paris. That's why I don't bother putting any deep roots here. What's the point; I want to travel bright, at the speed of light. And in order to do that, I don't need baggage. I look at the girls in my class, preening themselves, pouting into their shiny round hand-mirrors, making themselves ready for their dates, and I think, "Better you than me." Christ. I would rather die than be like them. That prince they're watching pull his rabbit out of a hat is only a toad in disguise. A toad – and a fraud. No real magic to lend its helping hand here, no magic at all. But they can't see this. They're already caught, hook, line and sinker. No escape. Game over.

'You're just jealous,' says my sister. 'Because you're not getting any.'

'Oh and you are? Tell me, Teodora, do Mum and Dad know their younger daughter is a slut?'

'You sad child!'

With that, and a flick of her resplendent ebony locks, my sister leaves the scene. 'You are the sad one,' I shout after her. 'You're just like everyone else!'

Teodora is two years younger than me, and she is what you'd call a popular girl. Her popularity is down to the most sickening mixture of things, like for instance:

a) ever since she was four years old, she pushed prams with random screaming babies up and down our street so that their mothers, as well as the rest of our neighbourhood, could complete an uninterrupted leg of daily gossip;

b) she was a young pioneer with the brightest eyes and sunniest smile, always rushing to throw flowers at our friend Tito as his convoy sped through another godforsaken town en route to some place far more important;

c) she never hides in the shed when our relatives pay us a visit; instead, she whips out her accordion and entertains the shit out of them for hours on end;

d) she always was, and still is a yes-girl. Not so much with me, but with everyone else. She's a born participator. Joiner. Part of a solution. A team player. Any team – she's on it, and

e) although she's a secret slut, Teodora successfully maintains her status of a girl's girl. She has a shitload of silly friends, they're forever phoning her, and popping in, and having sleepover parties. My mum made Dora invite me once, but I refused to go. Obviously. I stayed in my room watching pirated video copies of Last Exit to Brooklyn and Drugstore Cowboy – a depressing duo perhaps, but far less depressing than spending an entire evening amongst a group of squeaky girls making each other over in powder pinks and blues, talking jocks' cocks and mouthing out pigeon English versions of Mili Vanilli and Lisa Stansfield's so-called songs.

I wouldn't mind Teodora so much if I didn't have to live with her. This town is full of Teodoras, great and small, but I reckon it is a particularly bad luck to have one living under the same roof as me.

'Why did you have to go and procrastinate again, Daddy, when you already had me? You didn't need Teodora, that horrid little beast.' I was only, like, four, and I never understood why Dad used to find this question, presented to him in earnest, so funny he would just laugh and laugh, without ever remembering to give me a proper answer. 'Come on, darling,' he said. 'Let me buy you an ice cream for being my clever little girl!' I was pleased about the ice cream, also about being his clever little girl, but I remained thoroughly puzzled when it came to the actual reason for Teodora's existence. Especially as they already had me. I watched Dad eat his triple chocolate cone, and I wondered if grown-ups in general may be just too greedy for their own good. But more importantly, I realised that there was no point in asking a question if all you in return was an ice cream, and decided that, from then onwards, I would answer all the questions that pop into my head all by myself.

And that's precisely what I did.

'I don't think you should pour any more booze on top of the tetanus shot,' Iva told me just before we left her house. 'Mum says one of the possible side effects could be a full blown delirium.'

'I do like the sound of it.'

'Don't you dare!'

'Did you see that needle? Well, did you? Massive. And you know I have a fear of sharp objects. I deserve a drink, end of.'

A car drives around the corner. I put up a thumb. The driver pretends not to see me, no surprises there as he has a battle-axe of a wife is sat beside him. Iva and I are hitchhiking to Medison nightclub in Dalj, a village about half an hour away from Vukovar. I don't know why we keep returning to that dive, apart from the fact it stays open until the early hours, and serves alcohol right through. Other than that, it's a really depressing place, frequented by that typical socialist mix of criminally insane, small time politicians, proper genuine peasants (to be avoided at all cost), and last but not least – artists. There're always going to be artists in a place like that, because the creative light requires a steady flow of darkness in order to survive. This cool thought came to me out of nowhere roughly about three months ago, and I've been sharing it with anyone with ears ever since.

The best thing about Medison is that it has its own house DJ who, despite the demeanour of a freshly dug out potato, proves totally unprejudiced when it comes down to music, and takes great pride in playing every, I mean every, request taken, including those major crowd displeasers such as Bauhaus, The Cure and The Sisters of Mercy.

I love owning the dance podium with 'This Corrosion', or 'Boys Don't Cry', knowing full well that most of the fuckers lurking about in the gloom will never get this music, and therefore will never get me – not even if they tried for a thousand years, not even if they actually knew how. It feels good, dancing alone, or maybe with Iva, or one of the artist boys, it feels safe to know that the people watching me were not like me, and I could never become like one of them.

'I do worry about you.' Iva is leaning against an old plane tree in front of Count Eltz's Museum. 'I really do.'

'And why's that?'

'The way you rebel against everything, it's getting way out of control,' says Iva. 'I blame your parents, you know.'

'And so do I, I blame them for everything.'

'I'm being serious, Helena! The liberal parenting can be very neglectful of child's emotional needs. I read about it when I was researching my psychology essay.'

'Dad read me Shakespeare at bedtime, how's that for neglectful?'

'You do know the difference between intellect and emotions, right?'

I affect a yawn. 'How about you stop trying to psychoanalyse me and take your turn hitchhiking? My thumb is getting bored.'

It's early June. The night is warm, the skies are starry. We have two bottles of red wine safely netted in my bag, courtesy of Iva's father, or rather – his wine cellar. Mr Balić collected many things, most of them worse than useless, like stamps and match boxes and, double giggidy, fancy paper napkins, but it was his amazing wine collection that made me thank God for putting a nerd into the guy. Goes without saying, we help ourselves to his treasure only when we absolutely have to, on account of being broke and thirsty, which tends to happen no more than it's absolutely necessary for our survival.

I was a bit apprehensive the first time Iva took me down to the cellar. 'What if we take a really expensive bottle like a thousand billion deutschmark worth of wine, and he, like, notices?' I was slightly tipsy at the time, plus I'd had a couple of joints which made me feel super-paranoid, but also as sexy as sex on legs. 'What if he's got cameras, watching our every move, and he's phoning the police as we speak?'

'I hate it when you smoke,' said Iva. 'You go all demented. And will you stop rubbing yourself against me?'

'You wish!' I scanned the place for cameras. 'Hurry up, before he brings us down, way downtown.'

'Relax, you fool, his knee's too fucked to make it down the steps. Or up,' said Iva. 'Besides, he gets his buzz from buying the bottles, not counting them, and definitely not from drinking the wine. You know he's been teetotal for, like, ever.'

'Right. That makes sense.' I lie. 'I'll relax.'

Iva wasn't exactly stupid, but she sure was naïve. Relax? Even the song goes, Relax, don't do it. Meaning, keep yourself in a perpetual state of over-alert, or else.

'Dad must never know about this,' said Iva. 'It would break his heart to find out his only daughter was stealing from him.'

'Of course. What you don't know about only makes you stronger.'

It's all good, really. Just like this night. We have everything we need to get by. We have the wine, we have each other, we have enough cigarettes to smoke a bat out of hell, and I even found some cash in the back pocket of my jeans. How it survived the night of debauchery and zombie-babies I will never know. I count the notes. 'Weird. I have a feeling this is the exact same amount I stole from Teodora's room before I went out.'

'So how did you manage to get wasted?'

'I don't know. Maybe someone's spiked my drink.'

'What, like they do in the movies?'

'Yeah, exactly like–' I realise Iva's taking a piss. 'Oh come on! Vukovar may be a shithole, but it's also is a minor port, and those Bulgarian sailors are forever hawking their narco shit around town. Call yourself a detective's daughter!'

Iva's gaze's fixed at some place behind me. 'Talking of which…'

I turn to see a police car, kerb crawling right up my ass. A young policeman behind the wheel beckons Iva over.

'Come on!' Iva pushes me towards the car. 'We have ourselves a lift.'

Iva sits in front, I dive into the back seat. The young guy gives Iva's thigh a lingering squeeze. They think I don't see it, but I do. I feel a bit disappointed with Iva. What the fuck is she up to. Never took her for a dark horse. I check out the guy, give him a proper investigative once over. Blond, pretty, smiley, short. Kind of happy looking. Definitely not my type. Not much older than us, either. A mere boy in a starched blue uniform. Have I mentioned Jimi Hendrix is blasting out of the radio. What's that all about.

'Miki, Helena. Helena, Miki,' says Iva. 'Got any smoke?'

'What do you take me for? Of course I got smoke.' Miki starts patting himself down, in proper police fashion. It's hilarious to watch, but also a bit mind-numbing. 'Fuck. I forgot. I smoked it all this morning.' He catches me in the rear-view mirror. 'You! Tall girl. Duck!'

25

I only half-duck, resentful of the fact he called me a tall girl. Miki turns up the volume, puts on the siren, slams on the flashing blue light: Houston, we have lift-off.

STRANGER IN A STRANGE LAND

Miki pulls up at a roadside cafe in Borovo Selo. Serbian folk music is blaring out of the wide-open windows. How very embarrassing. Iva and Miki go in, I stay put and spy on the village women, clad in black, sitting on benches in front of their houses, watching fuck all go by. I call them Stone Women, have done since I was little, but maybe not in so many words.

I remember this one time, must've been like a million years ago, we drove through one of the villages on our way to a Sunday family gathering in Osijek.

'Look! An old man sitting on the bench!' said Teodora. 'Look! And another one!'

'Well spotted, Dora,' said my mum. 'Well done.'

Grown-ups miss just about everything. But I knew my sister was up to no good. She basically never was.

'But… Daddy?' She put on her whiney little girl voice, which normally made me want to hit her the worst. 'May I ask you a question?'

'Of course you may, darling.'

Teodora started to twirl a lock of hair around her forefinger, like she was trying to seduce her own dad, or something. She went, 'Well, isn't it a bit silly of Helena to call the people on the benches Stone Women, if there are also men sitting there?'

Dad cleared his throat. He did this to avoid giving an answer that might cause controversy. More than anything else in the world, Dad hated controversy, as well as things like conflict, argument, disagreement and dispute. In fact, he hated everything with potential to force his boat off the international-waters-only course. Just then, I spotted a bench with two men and a woman sitting on it.

'Daddy, look!' I pointed. 'Three Stone Women!'

'Daddy!' Teodora cried. 'Helena is teasing me again!'

'Calm down, Dora,' said Mum. 'She's not doing anything to you, not this time.'

'Yes, she is! There are two men on that bench, she can't call them the Stone Women! Daddy! Make her stop!'

'That's enough, Teodora!' Dad's voice came out like a thunder. 'You're to stop behaving like a spoilt brat, and let your sister use her imagination as she bloody well pleases!'

I've never heard my dad shout like that, before or since, and I'll never forget how happy that made me feel, it almost justified the fact I had a sister in the first place.

A loud knock on the window brings me back from my pleasant reverie.

It's Iva. 'His dealer's on his way. May as well have a drink. They have live music, with a proper half-naked singer from Niš, it's like nothing you've ever seen before.'

I need a pee, so I trail in. Christ. The place is full of old men, probably in their like fifties, so proper ancient. They all seem a) a bit drunk, and b) pathetically in love with the singer. Iva was right, I have never seen anything like this before in my life. Platinum blond bombshell. How often do you get to use this sentence on a real-life deal. I can't take my eyes off of her, the singer I mean. She is, like, two metres tall, and built like an Amazonian warrior, except she has both of her breasts intact. And when I say breasts, I mean zeppelins. She's wearing thigh-high faux-leather boots, silver edition, and a sparkly ripe apricot dress that just about stretches between her monumental ass and the said breasts. Her lips are as red as a gashing wound, she licks them little and often, like a grass snake. Her eyes are bluer than a baby boy's, she flashes them at me as I enter the room, and I swear they turn black for a moment, before she realises I'm no match for her game and turns back to being the perfect money-making machine. I kind of understand why these men are going crazy, slapping banknotes all over her sweaty rump and décolletage, and basically want to come into their pants there and then, except they can't because they're too old. She is sexy, if you like that sort of thing. And if you can put up with the noise that comes out of her. Kind of throaty, but not in a good way. Unless you're happen to be into frog concertos. Looking at these men, wouldn't put it past them.

I notice one of the musicians, a bald gypsy bass player, giving me far more than my fair share of a gold-toothed smile. Fuck this. I turn to Iva. 'I've had enough. Let's get the hell out.'

She hands me a bottle of beer. 'But I just bought you a drink.'

I feel a jolt in my stomach. Like anger, except I don't think I'm angry right now. 'Okay, a quick one, then we're off, yeah?'

Iva isn't listening to me. Too busy snogging the policeman. The music stops. I drink as much beer as I can in one go without too much gagging. The singer walks up to the bar.

'Give me your finest glass of water, bartender,' she says, in a super-stretched Belgrade drawl. Not Niš – Belgrade. Get it right, Iva. Who cares, anyway. What the fuck am I doing here, I should be some place better, some place elsewhere at the very least. I suddenly feel very disappointed with myself, and my so-called life. This world here, it's a bit too much for me to take in, too little to hang onto. I throw up, quick and easy, and all over those shiny, shiny silver boots of fake leather.

'It must've been the tetanus jab,' I say. 'I don't get on so well with medicines.'

Iva shoots me a nasty look. 'It's the beer you don't get on with. People like you should never be allowed to drink.'

We are walking towards Medison, having had to hitchhike the last leg of our journey. Miki got a bit upset, said I ruined his reputation. Told Iva he'll see her again when she starts keeping a more mature company. What age does he think she is, that moron. And now Iva's behaving as if any of the above was my fault. All I did was to go with the flow. I really don't get people sometimes.

The only bright cloud on my bleak, increasingly narrowing horizon was the fact the singer didn't seem all that upset with me, despite what I did to her boots. Alright, she did kind of grimace, like, 'Eeew!', but what she actually said to me was, 'What are you doing here, girl?' She messed up my carefully assembled fringe, added, 'Don't let me catch you in a place like this again, or I'll kick your skinny little ass all the way home, understood?' I managed to nod, before the bartender shooed me out of the door. Imagine. Being barred from a village bircuz at a tender age of sixteen.

I blame Iva.

I jump out of the cabin and wave off the friendly Hungarian lorry driver who helped Iva and me negotiate the last leg of our so-called journey. Iva buggers off towards Madison, I fall back, feeling sick and reluctant. A brand new white Merc pulls up into a driveway. Out of it jumps my sister, wait till I tell Mum and Dad, followed by a gaggle of her ugly girlfriends.

'What's up, sis?'

'Don't call me that!' Teodora doesn't seem too pleased to see me. 'How did you get here, on your broomstick?'

'Funny,' I lie. 'I hitchhiked, of course.'

'Seriously?' She makes a yuck-face. Not that she needs to try much. 'You're such a piece of a white trash it's unreal.'

Her flock falls about laughing. I stare at her for a second. Is she really that stupid. 'Teodora?'

'What?'

'You do realise that you and I are related, right…?' With that, I'm out of there. Let them ponder it out. Maybe they'll get it, eventually. Or maybe I should've made it easier for them, and said, 'So if I'm a piece of a white trash, what does that make you?' Or something equally as obvious. Arghh. What's the point, if you have to labour it to death.

If I didn't know better, I'd say I'm feeling mightily pissed off right now. Nothing in particular, just this sense of wanting to smash something to bits. Not that I would, though. I'd be too afraid I might hurt my hands. Or have a shard of the smashed thing ricochet straight into my eye, blind me to death. I hate a lot of things around here, but most of all I hate destruction. Not to mention conflict. Guess I get that from Dad. My dad and I, we totally share the love of international waters, should've been born Swiss. Not for us, the bloodthirsty Balkan land.

Think I need a drink.

Iva said I'd already had enough. What's up with that. I have barely even started, plus beer doesn't count, plus I lost most of it at the feet of that very nice lady singer. Wish she was my mother. Bet I'd feel much less neglected if she was my mum. And I bet that Dad would too.

I stroll down the road, find Iva chatting shit with a group of arty types of undisclosed creative persuasion; bit embarrassing for her, I know, but hey – whatever gets you through the night. I pull out a cigarette. A gun-shaped lighter appears as if from nowhere, right in front of my nose, all lit up and ready to go. I lean in, light up, then move on without bothering to check out the owner of the helpful yet highly intrusive hand. Probably just another hopeful peasant who saw me dancing my blues away and now wants to get a piece of the action. Arghhh. Peasants. They're so dumb.

'Hey, Iva, wouldn't it be fun if my sister, like, got together with one of the local peasants, then got pregnant and had to marry him and live in a trailer in his parents' yard? For the rest of her days? With chickens?'

'What are you on about?'

Iva acts all puzzled, like she has no idea what the fuck I'm on about, like she doesn't adore my surrealist drifts, and like I'm some idiot friend she only let tag along because both of our parents paid her. Can I believe her attitude? No I cannot.

I think for, like, a second. For Iva to act baffled by anything I say can only mean one of two things:

a) she's still pissed off at me about the Borovo Selo Incident, even though it's been at least a couple of hours since it passed, or

b) she wants me to fuck off so she can handpick one of the new boys, without running the risk of him falling for her prettier, more intense friend, i.e. yours truly.

Whatever it is, I hate her for it. I would support my friend no matter what kind of nonsense dribbled down her chin, and no matter how much better looking she was than me. So I walk away. I don't know where I'm going, I just don't want to be next to Iva. Or Teodora. Or the dance floor. Or outside, amongst the crowd spilling onto lawns two houses wide on each side of the club. I keep on walking until there's hardly anyone around. Then I stop. In a middle of the road. Road to nowhere. Which reminds me of Talking Heads. I like Talking Heads. I sing, We're on road to nowhere, come on inside, taking that ride to nowhere—

Somebody behind me claps. Nice one, Helena, going off like that, getting yourself followed, raped and killed by a bunch of mother fucking hillbillies. I turn around, part of me ready to jump out of my own skin, another part of me watching the jumpy part, thinking, "Thank FUCK I'm not this girl! So pathetic, she is, glad she's finally getting her comeuppance!"

'Hi there,' says this guy. I can just about make out his face in the moonlight. I kid you not about the moonlight, that's what happens here in the wilderness, the moonlight rules. He looks faintly familiar. Handsome, in a black and white movie kind of way. Needless to say, not my type. But not a pillaging villager, either, thank fuck, and I can't wait to try and pronounce this when I'm less stone cold sober. 'Nice night for it.'

I say nothing, just in case he missed the bit where he so rudely interrupted my rendition of 'Road To Nowhere'. I was really getting into it and everything. Oh the embarrassment, it burns. I reach for my trusty cigarette pack. The gun-shaped lighter reappears in front of my nose. I feel like I ought to make a stalker joke, but hand on heart, I'm not sure I can even be bothered. So what if there's a gun-shaped lighter wielding psycho tailing me. It's a free fucking country – or so they say.

'Hello, stalker.' Damn. I thought I just decided not to go there. 'What are you planning to do to me?' Double damn. Followed by exclamation mark.

He laughs. His laughing voice sounds like a male Tinkerbelle, if that makes sense. Well to me it does. 'I don't know – what would you like me to do to you?'

He also sounds kind of clever. And the other side of the river. Lots of Serbs come to Dalj, only a jump and a skip away across the Danube. I don't actually know any Serbian-Serbs, guess they kind of keep themselves to themselves. Especially these days. Everyone's talking politics, these days. And digging out the rifles that had been buried at the back of the garden for, like, decades, polishing them ready for some serious neighbour on neighbour blood spillage. People are so stupid. They are. That's why they never learn. It's exhausting to watch.

Apparently, there's an Apocalypse brewing out there. And I mean Apocalypse. But not right now, not this very moment. I look at the man, for that's what he is, a man. As opposed to a boy. Which is lucky, because I'm not terribly fond of boys, ever since one had almost cost me my entire sex life. I was only, like, too young to even mention when this boy from my class suggested that we should meet behind the gym and learn how to kiss and cuddle like grown-ups. We did it once. I wasn't at all convinced, so we did it again. And again. It took seven heavy petting sessions altogether for me to decide that I was done with this particular way of wasting my time. A couple of years later, I accidentally bumped into this random man at Nama supermarket: as he grabbed my shoulders to help steady me, I got hit by the biggest muskiest scent that instantly jellified my legs and made my pulse race out of orbit. Easily the biggest eureka moment in my life. Think I was even in love, for about five minutes it took me to follow my mystery man to a parking lot where his fat wife gave me the dirtiest look known to woman-kind. My desire vanished as suddenly as it had appeared; like a bat out of hell went I, but a totally transformed bat at that.

'Maybe,' I say. 'You'd like to smell the back of my neck?'

Yeah I know: I sound like the opening sentence of one of those paperback novelettes Mum keeps in a wooden crate under the sink. She doesn't want Dad to see them. I wish I hadn't seen them, either. I'm not too proud of having a mother who reads that sort of crap. Thank God for Daddy. Like I tried to tell Iva earlier, my bedtime stories, always delivered by Dad, were a mixture of Greek mythology, Shakespeare and, his firm favourites:

a) stories of Serbia's triumph over the Ottoman Empire, and

b) stories of Russia's triumph over the German invaders in WW2.

Saying that, I'm even less keen on having a mother who thinks she has to hide her stuff from her husband. That's kind of sad. If I were to read crap, I'd make sure everyone knew about it. Including my husband. Not that I'll ever marry.

The man comes right up close. 'I would.'

I breathe in his scent, deep, all the way to my knees. 'You smell like an earthworm.'

His laughter makes my heart feel glad. Odd, that. He places his hand at the back of my head, gently draws me in. 'You're lovely.'

A couple of cars come out of nowhere, and pull in front of us. A door swings open, Iva pops out her head. 'Chop-chop Helena, there's a party we must attend to!'

I hesitate. Mostly on account of my present dislike of Iva, but also because I don't want to leave the man with the gun-shaped lighter. 'I'm bringing a friend!'

He squeezes my arm. 'Stay with me.'

Iva shakes her head. 'No can do. We're already bursting at the seams.'

I look at the stranger. 'Stay,' he whispers.

'Sorry,' I say. 'Gotta go.'

He steps back into the darkness. Suddenly there's so much room around me. Too much bloody room. I feel dizzy. Thirsty. Iva's grin is splitting her face into two. The boys in the car all look the same, with their silver skin and under the radar gaze. Some people believe that there isn't such thing as a wrong choice, only a false one. I curl up onto someone's lap. The car peels off into the night. Somebody lights up a joint. It is time to try and forget it's ever happened.

What's ever happened.

MAKING FRIENDS
&
INFLUENCING PEOPLE

'Who the fuck are you?'

I open my little eye and spy an old woman, sitting on the bed next to me. She clocks I'm awake, gets to her feet, starts saying random stuff and waving her arms about. Just like a human windmill. I can tell she's not an immediate threat to me, though. So I pay her no more heed and instead concentrate on checking my present whereabouts.

Nope. Never seen this place before in my life. If I were to become a murder suspect in a police inquiry right now, and they were to plug me into a lie detector to check whether I've ever visited the victim in their home, I would go, 'I swear on my life, or something, I have never been to that person's house, officer!', and pass with flying colours. Because, although I am here, I'm also kind of certain that:

a) I was never here,

b) I am not here now, and

c) I will never come here again.

'Where am I?' I ask the woman. 'I mean, where in the world?'

She stops talking. Progress is good. I get out of bed and stretch. Christ. Stiff as a board. And kind of peckish. The woman starts crying. I really wish she wouldn't.

'Er,' I say. 'What's the matter?'

She makes this dramatic sweeping motion towards the bed with one arm, and with other, I kid you not, she covers her eyes. There's a sound of a key turning in the door, must be Charlie Chaplin to the rescue. I light a cigarette, mmmm, tastes so good. Iva walks in, followed by a very tall man with a long black hair. Being him looks like a struggle to me, like he wants to grow up, but his hair wants to grow down; a vertically challenged tug of war. He drops a brown paper bag he's holding, so surprised he is to see the woman snivelling in the corner. Crash, goes the bag.

'Silvia! When did you come back?'

She grabs an important looking tome from a shelf and throws it in his general direction. I duck a little, but there's no need: she throws like a girl. The book hardly even lifts off before hitting the floor dead. Silvia yelps in pain. The weight of the book must've dislocated the wrist on her so-called throwing hand. I'm guessing she may be far too old and brittle for such attempts of violence. I spy a lonely glass perched on the very edge of the sideboard. I instinctively know it is half filled with vodka not water and make a beeline.

'You fucking bastard,' says Silvia. 'I only left a week ago! And already, you have orgies! With underage girls!'

'I'm forty-one,' I say.

'No, no, no…' The guy's hands are trembling. He must be either in love or terrified. Iva's picking up the pastries that fell out of the bag. I down the vodka. It's action stations all around. 'This is Iva, you know – Ratko's daughter. She came to our meeting last night, wants to become proactive within the party… Except,' and here he turns to me, as does everyone else. Just when I was about to sneak off in search of more vodka. I freeze. 'Her friend here, well it's a very funny story, because the poor darling drank one spritzer too many, so naturally I felt like I had no choice but to let them stay. Mea culpa, mea culpa, I shouldn't have let her drink at all, she's terribly allergic to alcohol, isn't that right, Iva?'

The woman stares at me with those dead eyes of hers. 'She doesn't look like a poor darling to me!'

'Oh but she is! Don't let her wild appearance fool you,' says my long-haired host. 'She's extremely vulnerable, physically, as well as,' here he lowers his voice a 'why even bother' tiny bit. 'Mentally. Iva didn't want to deliver her home in such a state. Helena's parents are very strict.'

'Who the fuck are you?' I say. 'And who are you calling vulnerable? And stop talking about my parents like you know them, because you don't, you lying moron!'

I am not an aggressive person per se, but this guy is making me want to kill him. Listening to his whining, it's just too embarrassing. And all the excuses, just so he gets himself off the hook – not exactly noble, is he, not exactly a hero.

He straightens up from his begging for mercy

stance and is now towering over me like some very ugly dick. 'Iva? Please ask your friend to leave. Before I do something I may later regret in court.'

Ask me to leave? Me? And what's up with his glib play on words, was that a threat? Surely, this man should be put down. Failing that, stopped. I look at Iva, but for some reason she seems to be giving me daggers. Me – not him. 'Helena...'

'Say no more,' I say. 'I'm outta here.' I grab my battered satchel off the nightstand and look for my boots. Both things are the favourite parts of my uniform, all scruffy brown leather and no frills, to go with everything else I wear. And everything else is black, so not even I can tell the difference when it comes to what I'm wearing from one day to another. As I pull on the boots I wink at the woman, then say, in a sort of a loud whisper you'd need to be stone deaf not to pick up, 'Beast in bed, for sure. I don't blame you for hanging on.' I deliver this pitch-perfect, except for beast bit, I almost burst out laughing there. And suddenly it's mayhem. The man goes, 'You little bitch!' and throws himself at me, but misses by a mile because I'm not only prepared for every eventuality, but also dead quick on my feet and no one's ever managed to catch me yet. I jump over the bed, he jumps after me, hits the headboard, the dick's head bursts open, there's blood everywhere, game over. The woman stops throwing random things in random directions and is now crying blue murder in a most unattractive way. Iva's shouting things at me, I do not understand a word. She eventually drags me away by the scruff of my jacket, but not before I manage to

41

grab a lonely looking wallet from a console table in the hallway, and then we're out of there.

After a block or two, I start to feel a bit too out of breath for my liking. Teodora's dead fond of Jane Fonda and aerobics, and is forever puffing and panting to a video tape. I find the notion of resembling Teodora in any way, shape or form, even accidentally, a little upsetting to say the least. So I slow down. Iva's rushing ahead like a woman possessed, looking like she knows where she's going. I am not sure where we are going. Or even where we are. Vukovar it ain't. Nor Vinkovci. So Osijek, or maybe Zagreb. Once I woke up in Sarajevo, at this unfamiliar guy's place, and just rolled with it. His accent soon informed me of my whereabouts. That, and the fact that his place was on the Jahorina mountain. He gave me a wolf cub called Rea. For real. I brought it home, but my dad wouldn't let me keep it. I have never seen him so mad. But it was all one big misunderstanding, because my parents were supposed to be away on holiday for a week, not only three days. Then my mum went and developed a major toothache, didn't she, so they had to come home early. Really not my fault I was missing in action for the following two days. Anyway, it was poor Rea who got excommunicated instead of me, and made to earn her keep on some chicken farm. At first I hoped she would kill all the chickens, but then I changed my mind, on account of what would happen to Rea if she really went and caused such carnage. They'd probably skin her alive. Adults. I'm not all that keen on them. The stuff they get up to, it's criminal.

'Iva!' She doesn't answer, doesn't slow down. I catch up with her, despite the major shortage of breath causing all my internal organs to declare a state of emergency. 'Iva! Slow down! Fuck!'

She stops, turns on me, 'What the fuck do you want?'

I actually have no answer to this.

'Do you realise Vladimir let you sleep in his house, in his bed, for the last two days?'

'Two days?' My parents are going to disown me. Unless I manage to lay my hands on another wolf cub. Perhaps I could steal someone's cat, perhaps a cat would do.

'Yes! And this is how you repay him?'

'My dad's going to kill me.'

'Well I hope so, you selfish little cunt!' Iva walks into a deserted playground, located underneath the most deliciously scented linden tree canopy. She sits on the swing and lights up. I sit next to her. My swing's broken, so I need to stay on my toes. 'We drove to Osijek Saturday night, after Dalj. Remember? Do you buggery. Such a fucking liability, you are. Well anyway, we did, we came here to watch all fourteen episodes of Berlin Alexanderplatz back to back.'

'Oh yes, I remember that.'

Iva snorts. 'You liar. You went straight for Vladimir's bed, it was so weird, total autopilot, like you knew exactly where it was, and within five seconds you were snoring. Didn't move a muscle until this morning.'

'No wonder I feel stiff.'

'I phoned your house, told them you were at mine, helping me with some course work. Your mum fell for it, so you're in the clear.'

Not surprised my mum lapped it up. She reckons Iva is the dumbest amongst my not very numerous friends. 'It's the thick one,' she would say if Iva phoned and she happened to answer. Iva didn't like my mum, either. I don't know why this happens, some people are just not meant to be together, not even on the same planet.

'So we're in Osijek. Great. Glad it's not Zagreb, or worse.' I'm just shooting the breeze here. Making sure the conversation's flowing away from criticising Helena. 'And I'm sorry if I've offended your friend.'

'My friend?'

'Yeah. Vladimir.'

'He isn't really my friend,' says Iva. 'He's just a guy.'

We swing in silence for a few minutes. I'd kill for a bottle of ice cold Coca-Cola. I finger the stolen wallet in my bag, dead surreptitious. I can feel a fat wodge of cash nesting inside. Yet I'm shy to show it to Iva. Vladimir may be just a guy, but he knew Iva's dad, and he mentioned some party... Doubt he meant spin the bottle eat the cake strip naked for the boys kind of a party, I suspect some sort of a hush-hush political situation. There's more to this than meets the eye for sure, as very old people would say. I decide to keep schtum about the wallet. Which means hunger, thirst and hitchhiking back to Vukovar.

Fucking Vukovar. All the effort that goes into

leaving it, only to have to return again. Hardly worth it, but I have no better idea at this point in time. No other design for living.

'So,' I say. 'We don't have any cash, is that right?'

Iva glances towards my satchel. My heart jumps. I like stealing, but hate getting caught. Especially by your usual partner in crime. 'Do you have anything in there?'

'Nope.'

'Well then we have none.'

'Fuck da police.'

'Why did you say that?'

I shrug. 'I don't know.'

She jumps off the swing, hits the dust running. I go after her. 'What's up?'

She stops, stares deep into my eyes. I wonder if this is where I kiss her, because that is how the story goes, right: first we stare at each other's eyes, then we kiss, then we marry, than we have kids and then we die, unless we were dead all along, in which case no grand finale for us, oh no. Iva flicks my left brow. Ouch. 'You're so weird, you know that?' She speeds off, shouting, 'Come on, let's find Mr Ferlan, see if he'll buy us breakfast.'

DADDY DEAREST

Only people with no imagination went to study at Osijek University. The choice of courses was as fun as its clientele: Law, Teaching, Economy, Food Technology, Agricultural Studies; need I go on. Dad used to work for the government, not sure what job, exactly, have a feeling he might've been a spy. He hated it, though, so when they opened the university in Osijek back in the seventies, he was like, I'm going to teach now, and there's nothing anyone could do to stop him. So he now teaches at the Law school, and the Economy school, and sometimes he teaches at the Teaching school. Not sure what his actual subject is. Never bothered to ask, and he never bothered to say. Anyway. Today is supposed to be Monday, which means he's at the Law school. I'm not all that ecstatic about this begging mission, but what else am I supposed to do. Question mark. I did consider getting accidentally separated from Iva, so I could freely feast with the wallet-money. Except she's now slowed right down and is walking real close to me, chatting shit and being generally too friendly to ditch.

The staff room's almost empty. A couple of old men are sitting at the table, but don't even look up when Iva and I stroll in. I help myself to a couple of handfuls of cherries from the bowl. Pass one to Iva. We walk around empty corridors, spitting stones onto the marble floor, watch them bounce about, leaving red juice marks in their wake. It's quiet. I imagine the two of us as the only people left in the world after God smote the rest of the population into nothingness. I glance at Iva, skulking about in her usual uniform of jet black jump suit and long, bleached bone-in-a-desert white hair, all piled haphazardly on top of her head. A proper comic book heroine. Would fit into most end of the world scenarios. Yet only a year ago I had to sit her down and explain real slow why it was not cool to be seen dead in the baby blue dungarees and foam-banana yellow cardigan type of gear her German cousins kept sending her for every birthday since she was two.

'You must tell them to stop presenting you with this *scheisse*,' I said, as gently as I could. 'Ask them to send you money instead.'

She caressed the clothes I piled up against a wall, ready for execution. 'But they are such good quality things… Lacoste. Benetton. Touch them – so soft. Go on, touch them.'

Well I wouldn't touch them. I was kind of starting to lose my patience with Iva at that point of our relationship. It was only a matter of time before I started to call her my pastel-by-proxy phase, and move on. But two weeks later, Iva showed up in front of school wearing a shiny black boiler suit, black winkle-pickers and super-bleached hair that took my breath away.

She walked up to me, same old/same old, shut my mouth with a little flick of her forefinger against my lower jaw, said, 'They gave me the money.'

My hair being naturally as black as the raven's armpit, it didn't take long before one exceptionally witty student thought up of calling us Ebony and Ivory. Needless to say, in town where very few things dare to stand out, our new nicknames spread like wildfire. I was of course called Ivory too often to even beggar belief, and Iva, hidden behind a long curtain of peroxide-induced pallor, kept batting back Ebony salutes with a curt, 'Fuck off, you blind cunt!' Must admit I secretly quite liked being one half of such a super-cool team. I never was a team player before, never dreamed of such horror, yet in reality, I enjoyed it almost as much as I hated to admit it. But would all of the above be enough to want to spend the rest of my life with only Iva for company?

I look at her again. She is loitering around the biggest houseplant I've ever seen. Her eye catches mine. 'Look away for a second, will you?'

I turn away. "What are you up to?'

'I'm changing my tampon.'

'Oh.'

'Almost there. Right, done. You can look again if you like.'

I slowly turn. She's digging up the dirt around the plant. 'Tampon burial?'

'Yep.' Iva wipes her hands on her suit, gets to her feet. 'I'm cramping. Can you ask Professor if he has an Andol?'

'Sure.' I point to the wooden bench in the corner.

'Why don't you make yourself comfortable, it shouldn't be long now.'

Poor Iva. Pain is a horrible thing. I check the clock on the wall: another ten minutes. I do like hanging around, waiting for something to happen. The best part of any event is the before part. Loitering in anticipation. If there were such a thing as a Loitering School, I would actually consider working there. Part-time only, of course, I have no time for a so-called proper job. Or maybe I could open my very own College of High Class Loitering. Or Madame Helena's School of Sophisticated Heel Dragging. Bet it would prove to be a roaring success around these shores.

Iva, on the other hand, is not very good at loitering. I don't mean just now, I mean in general. She fidgets and shifts and huffs and puffs. I, on the other hand, loiter like a proper pimp. I do a lot of leaning, against my elbows if I'm sat with a table behind me, or against my shoulder blades if I'm stood up against a wall. Presently, it's the wall. I push my hips right out, then pull them in, so that my lower back hovers a few millimetres away from the wall, but never actually touches it. I swing my hips left and right a couple of times, then out they go again.

The bell sounds off. I drop the pimp attitude for one of true yet cheeky humility. Dad's real clever when it comes to human nature, must be all the spy training he'd received. Too humble, and he's on your case for being too proud. Too cheeky, and he's busting your ass for being too meek to say what you really mean. Tricky man, Dad. Hard to please.

The students start coming out, every single one of them looking none too keen on changing the world any time soon. I push through the last few, holding my breath in case I ingest their stagnatory staleness. The classroom is empty, except for some girl trying to seduce Dad – most of them do. The two of them seem to be engrossed in a story that would no doubt bore most people into a murder-suicide. But apparently not them.

There's a guy in the corner, struggling to either connect or disconnect a projector from a video player. Must be one of Daddy's little helpers. Surprised to see a man. Usually they're all women. 'A little sexual tension never fails to inspire creativity,' my dad would say. He'd then look at my mum, but she'd be too caught up with the romantic ups and downs of her paper-chain people to notice his so-called tease.

I walk over to the loser with the projector, say, 'Need some help?'

'That would be great, thanks.'

He turns around, but the sound of his voice has already made me go all high alert. 'What the fuck,' I say, 'are you doing here?'

The man from the road to nowhere is smiling at me. 'I work here.' He points at my dad. 'You?'

I suddenly feel really angry. It's as if everything I haven't had the time to feel wants to break loose and catch up with me, like, right this moment. Except the me it wants to catch up with has already moved on, and is busy chasing another clue to another place where another, better life awaits another better me. So no point in those stupid old feelings trying to get me, for I'm not even here.

I realise I'm staring at the man, standing here gaping like a fool with nothing better to do with her life. Without uttering another word, I turn on my heels and walk over to the desk where Dad's regaling the blondie with a story of the Battle of Stalingrad. 'Hi Daddy, can I please have some money so Iva and I can have a bite to eat? Also, she's lost our bus tickets. So could we please have even more money?'

He looks surprised, thank God pleasantly. Too pleasantly, in fact, because he makes a great big deal out of it. 'Darling! What a lovely surprise! Barbara, this is my daughter, Helena. Helena, meet Barbara, my star student.'

I shake the blonde girl's hand, it's small and clammy, and altogether disgusting, then give Dad a hug and plant myself by his right side. The man from Dalj joins us. I'm no longer angry, but now I feel like I'm about to pee myself. Christ. What is wrong with me.

'And this is Lazar,' says Dad. 'My right-hand and colleague. Lazar – Helena.'

More hand shaking. But Lazar's hand, it feels like coming home. Never liked this saying, but that's what it feels to hold Lazar's hand. I remember to let go just as the whole thing starts to edge towards plain awkward. 'Your father is being too generous, as usual. I'm but a humble assistant.'

Just then, Iva drags her sorry ass in. And I mean sorry. She's as pale as a sheet, barely standing up.

'Iva?' says Dad. 'You don't look too good, dear.' He helps her into a chair. 'What's the matter?'

Iva fixes a glassy stare on me. 'I need a painkiller.'

'Oh? Okay.' Dad turns to his start pupil. 'Barbara, would you–'

He doesn't even need to finish, Barbara's already out of the door. Good job, Daddy! When I grow up I'm going to get myself a slave and call it Barbara.

Lazar fetches a glass of water. 'Take a sip, it'll make you feel better.'

Iva looks up at him, smiles a little. Shit. What if Lazar likes Iva better than me? Just look at them. They seem to be getting along real well.

'It's only her period,' I say. 'She's not dying or anything.' All three of them look at me. 'In case you were wondering.'

Barbara bursts back onto the scene, bearing a whole strip of Andol. 'One? Two?'

'Four,' says Iva.

Barbara eyes my father, he nods his head. Christ. Is he like some kind of a Jesus figure around here. She hands over the tablets, Iva chases them down with a glass of water – you'd think that would be the end of it. But no. Fifteen minutes later, as we're munching through a hot cheese *burek* kindly procured by Barbara the Slave, and I'm on the verge of hitting it off with Lazar, Iva starts making noise.

'My stomach… It's burning…'

Dad turns to me. 'Has she eaten anything today?'

I shrug. 'How do I know?'

'Helena,' he goes. 'You're supposed to be her friend.'

He walks over to attend to Iva, Barbara hops off after him. Up to this moment, I was only picking at my *burek*, as I don't like eating in front of strangers.

But now I give up the game altogether and chuck the whole thing into the paper basket. I'm a good friend. I am. Dad is a bastard for saying something like that and I hate him for it.

'You alright?' says Lazar.

I nod. If I speak I will surely cry. I can't even look at him. I suspect his eyes are all kindly and deep, and I'm sure if I looked into them I would drown. So I don't speak, or look at him. Then suddenly I say, 'I want to go home.'

He leans in – I still can't quite look at him, except with my peripheral vision, says, 'And where is Helena's home?'

HOME & BOUND

I'm staring at the ruler-straight road as it unfolds in front of my eyes. Tiredness is pressing at my temples and making my nose itch. I have been out and about, back and forth, clockwise and anti-clockwise, but mostly anti, for the last four or five days. Admittedly, I did sleep through half of this time, but still, I feel exhausted. And guilty. Going home does this to me every time, without fail. I hate this guilt, must be the way I was programmed or something. My mum won't be saying much, besides, 'Oh, look who's back.' Dad, well, he's far too cool to tell me off, always has been. No wonder I grew wild.

But I digress. Inability to focus, it's practically worrying. I stare at the road even harder. Iva moans from the back seat.

'Are you okay?' asks Lazar.

'Yes,' she says, in that weak as a kitten voice she normally conjures up to get a day off school. Her mum always falls for it. Her dad just waves his hand. He doesn't care. I hope Lazar won't care either, hope he'll see straight through her manipulating ways. 'Do you happen to have a cigarette on you?'

Do you happen to...? What's up with the milk

maiden talk. Not that I've ever heard an actual milk maiden actually talk, but I bet this is exactly what they sound like: good and proper. And all other things Iva's not.

'You're not supposed to smoke,' I say. 'It'll only thin your blood.' I don't know what I'm talking about, but it sure sounds proper medical. 'Just go back to sleep.'

'Nonsense,' she says and picks herself up. Next thing, she's wrapped her arms around Lazar's seat. The poor man looks pretty uncomfortable right now, straining his neck away from her pretend oh-so-nonchalant physical arrangement. 'Helena can get so protective, it almost hurts.' She turns to me. 'Cigarette, please?'

I hand over a cigarette and keep schtum. Lazar saw me first. Hardly a coincidence. And if Iva wants to take on Destiny, then good luck to her (not).

'Nothing wrong with a bit of loyalty,' Lazar says. 'A girl after my own heart.'

Am I hearing things, or has Lazar just proposed to me. Iva must've heard it too, for she unwraps herself from his seat, and says, 'Yes, well... Helena can be very, what's the word? Lovable? When she so chooses.'

And still, I say nothing. I feel like a spiritual giant right now. *He, who cast the first stone...* No, that's not it. *Love is patient, love is kind, it lets thy neighbour make a fool out of her own self.* Yep. That's more like it.

'What kind of a name is Lazar, anyway?' Iva refuses to stay down. How embarrassing not to mention annoying. 'Are you a Serb?'

I cringe on the inside. Can't believe Iva's talking politics, *again*. I sneak a peek at Lazar. He does have a bit of an accent, but he doesn't look like a Serb to me. Then again, nor does my father, yet he's a Serb alright. My point being, they both look like everyone else. Okay, maybe not the people from Ethiopia, or China. What I mean is, Serbs look like Muslims, Muslims look like Croats, Croats look like Serbs, etc. They all sound exactly the same, too. So how can you tell. And why the fuck would you want to. I sneak another peek. This time, Lazar's waiting. There's a look in his eye I want to grab and run with, put it in a box, bury the box under the willow tree and sit on it forever. I suspect this is the exact opposite of marrying him, opposite to what most people would consider a happy ending. God. I feel like crying. But I'm happy, really.

'My father was a Greek,' he says. 'And my mother was a Macedonian.'

'Was?' I say. 'Were?'

'Yes – sadly, they both died. In a plane crash.'

Iva sneers. 'Yeah, right.'

How very insensitive. Exclamation mark.

'It's true,' he says. 'Air France Flight 1611 that crashed off Nice, after a fire in the cabin, killing all ninety-five on board. 1969. I was ten-years-old.'

I never know what you're supposed to do with tragedies. My own, other people's. Henry Miller, calmly stepping over a corpse on a Parisian street circa 1932, now this I do get. Shit happens, no point stressing over it. It's not like we can change the past.

So step over that corpse, then take another step. And another. Get the fuck out of there.

Just then, I spot a tractor in a distant field.

'That tractor doesn't have a driver,' I say. 'It's basically driving itself.'

'Shit,' says Iva. 'I'm so sorry.'

'It's called a technological advance,' I say. 'Supposed to be a good thing.'

Lazar looks in the rear-view mirror. 'Thank you, Iva. It happened such a long time ago, I hardly even remember them.'

Oh my God. Are we still talking the past.

'Still,' says Iva. 'You never get over something like that.'

Well I do. 'Did you, like, grow up in an orphanage?' I ask Lazar. 'Like Oliver Twist?'

Iva laughs. Poison Iva. 'Didn't I tell you Dickens was going to rot your brains? See? It's happened.'

'Shut up, Iva!' I feel upset. I feel very upset. I decide never to see Iva again after today. So glad I didn't actually kiss her when I thought she wanted me to.

She kicks my seat. 'Sensitive much?'

'Stop it!'

She kicks my seat again.

'Stop the car!'

'Oh, come off it,' says Iva.

'Really?' says Lazar.

'Really, really, stop the car, now!' I open the door, Lazar slams his foot on the brakes. I scramble out. 'Thank you.'

'Just leave her,' Iva's saying. 'Fucking baby.'

I walk back, kick her side of the car, then walk off again. Lazar catches up with me. 'Helena?' The car is milling alongside. I'm grateful he doesn't run me over. Why would he. I don't know. But I would, I'd run myself over right now, if only I could. 'Get back into the car. Please?'

I ignore him. I would like to say something, but I can't, because:

a) I don't want Iva to overhear, and

b) I feel like I'm sure to burst into tears if I utter even the tiniest of noises.

So we go on like this for a few minutes: I march along a grassy strip beside a dusty road, Lazar and his bad-seed-load kerb crawl behind. I can go on like this forever. See who wins. I barely take in a blue and white milicija car driving past in the opposite direction, until it turns around and pulls right up in front of me. The driver and passenger both jump out of the vehicle in a synchronised fashion of a cop comedy sketch, but this does very little to ease the sense of foreboding that suddenly spills inside my chest.

'Good morning,' says the taller policeman. 'Enjoying the walk?'

I nod. My attention is firmly focused on his brush-like moustache; I want to pluck it off his face and use it to polish my Dr Martins back into black. With a corner of my eye, I see the other policeman, short round ginger bloke, ordering Lazar out of the car.

'Your identity card,' says Moustache. 'Where did you say you were from?'

I didn't. 'I didn't.'

'Don't you go lippy on me,' says Moustache. 'Don't even think about it. Do you get what I'm saying?'

I get it. I start digging around my rucksack. My hands are trembling. I've heard very bad stories about rogue roadside policeman. Very bad stories indeed. Luckily, we have Iva with us, one mention of her father the police detective, and we'll be on our merry. Worked many times before, although I never wanted it to work this bad. Moustache's head crops up so close to my face I can actually feel his moustache breathe all over my left cheek. He softly growls, 'Do you get me, little girl?'

I look away, nod.

'Speak up!' he yells. 'Or have you left your tongue some place you shouldn't have?'

'Yes, I get you. Here.'

He snatches the identity card out of my hand, takes my hand with it, I pull it back. He's fixing me with his glassy blue eyes all along, in a way I never want to see anyone look at me again. I really wish Iva would make her influential presence felt, any time soon would do.

'What kind of a name is this, Lazar Angelis?' asks the ginger policeman, Ginge for short. 'Serbian, right? Your papers, please. And take it easy, because I'm keeping my eye on you, is that clear?'

'Absolutely.' Lazar reaches into the car, our eyes meet. He winks at me, then hands over the papers. 'It's a Greek name, by the way.'

'Same difference,' says Ginge. 'Don't you move an inch.' He marches back to the patrol car and starts making radio calls. I bet he's only pretending. I bet this is the only thing that makes him feel even a little bit important. That, and having it off with prostitutes. I yawn. I tend to yawn a lot when under pressure.

'Bored, are we?' Moustache whispers. I snap my mouth shut. 'Oh, don't stop... I really like the look of your tongue.'

'Ew,' I say.

'What did you say?'

'Nothing.'

And before I know what's hit me, Moustache has me spreadeagled on the bonnet of the car. 'I warned you, didn't I, I said do not to go lippy on me, little girl!' He forces himself behind me, I can feel his hand in between my legs. With his other hand, he's holding both of my arms locked up behind my back. 'You! Don't move!'

I hear Lazar's voice. 'What seems to be the problem, officer? What did the girl do?'

'I said, don't fucking move!' Moustache presses himself harder against me. I'm thinking of passing out, but no such luck. I'm just not a passing out kind of a girl.

'I'm not moving,' says Lazar. 'It's just that I have promised Helena's father, who is a professor at Osijek University, to bring his daughter home safe and sound. I feel responsible, so please tell me if there's anything I can do to help improve this situation.'

Moustache takes his hand off my crotch. 'You can shut the fuck up!' My relief proves to be a mixed blessing when he uses his newly freed hand to pull a gun out of a holster, and aim it at Lazar. 'Now get into the vehicle and drive the fuck away!'

'I'm not leaving without Helena.'

'Listen up, dickhead, I'm giving you this one last chance–'

'Whoa-whoa-whoa!' Ginge's voice sounds beyond alarmed. 'Mario? Put the gun down. Nice and easy now. Mario? Put it down!'

I can feel Moustache's dilemma. I really can. 'I'll put it down after Serb leaves. I let him go, fair and square. I have no bone to pick with him.' He presses on my arms, hard. 'But her I must keep for further investigation. I can tell she's a criminal.'

Lazar again, 'She is just a teenager. Harmless. I will vouch for her, I promise. Keep my papers if you like, and I'll take her home, and that'll be the last you'll ever hear from us.'

Ginge comes up close to Moustache. 'Have you lost your mind?' he hisses. 'Let go of the girl, man, before you get us both labelled with false imprisonment and molestation of a minor. Mario? I'm pulling rank here. Come on. Let's go see Big Berta, she's always good to go, come on, man, my treat.'

Moustache steps back, I slip to the ground. Lazar whips around the car, scoops me up into his arms. I hold on tight and we stand there, not taking our eyes off the two policemen. After helping Moustache back into the patrol car, Ginge walks over, his notepad ready. 'Sorry about my colleague. He's been under a lot of pressure. I'll make sure nothing like this ever happens to you again, Mr Angelis,' he says. 'I've taken a note of your registration plate, and I'll flag it to all our units. You'll be treated like a diplomat from now on, all green lights and school kids throwing flowers as you cruise on by.' His forced laughter hits the wall of silence. 'The times are hard, Mr Angelis. The war is coming, there's no stopping it now. Nothing personal, right? Please explain this to the girl, if you would. So she understands. Promise me you'll make sure she understands, and we'll be on our way.'

'I wanted to help,' says Iva. 'But I just couldn't, okay? I am sorry. Helena? Come in, have a drink, let's just chill the fuck out.'

We are parked in front of her house. I turn to Lazar. 'Can you please take me home?'

He nods. 'It's okay, Iva. Not your fault. Go and rest, I'm sure Helena will come around.'

We drive off. 'I won't, you know.'

'Won't what?

'I won't come around.'

'You will... Eventually.'

'I could've been–'

'But you weren't.'

'No thanks to that scaredy-cunt.'

Lazar laughs. 'I'm sure you don't mean it.'

'Oh but I do. She could've helped us, but she just sat there, I mean, what kind of a person does that?'

'You said it yourself – she was scared,' says Lazar. 'And who can blame her? I couldn't do anything, either.'

'At least you tried!'

'The most important thing is that, although the human race might have failed you, you still got all the help you needed.'

'What does that even mean?'

Lazar pulls up in front of my house, then turns to look at me. Even better, he cups my face in his hands and holds it there for a moment. 'I mean you are a very lucky girl, well looked after.'

Even though I dare not breathe for fear of spoiling the moment, I still have to ask, 'So are you my stalker, or something?'

But he doesn't pull away. 'I could be something... Couldn't I?'

'You're far too old.'

'Says who?'

'Says the bald patch on top of your head.' I grab my stuff and jump out of the car, and I never look back, although I really, really want to.

WOMEN WHO RUN AROUND VUKOVAR

That night, I decide the only thing left for me to do is to become a hermit.

'I'm not here for anyone, okay?' I inform the members of my so-called family the next morning. 'If anyone calls, or visits, or whatever, just tell them I'm out.'

'Out where?' asks Dad.

'Anywhere.'

'So,' he says. 'Would it be acceptable to tell your imaginary callers you're out in the fields, digging potatoes?'

Teodora sniggers.

'Dad!' This here is exactly why I'm becoming a hermit, people are just too I don't even know what; something that I'm not, for sure. 'All you need to say is that I'm out. No details, nothing.'

'Are you feeling alright, Lena?' asks Mum. Why go and call me Lena? She knows I hate being called that, kick me when I'm down why don't you. 'Why are you hiding? Who are you hiding from? It's a beautiful day, go out, frolic…!'

I can't believe she's just told me to go do the F-word. The woman's clearly so far up her own candyfloss dream she can't even fake interest. Telling me to go frolic is like telling a great white shark to go play nicely with a goldfish. Ambivalent mother, forgetful mother, my mother. No wonder I'm withdrawing from society at the tender age of, hum, who cares.

'Please don't call me Lena,' I say. 'By the way, what year was I born in?'

Mum and Dad look at one another.

'Right, it was, er...' That was Dad.

'Yes,' goes Mum. 'I think you're right.'

The telephone rings. Saved by the bell, my so-called parents. Teodora answers.

'Yeah, she's standing right here. No, she can't,' she says. 'Because she doesn't want to speak to anyone. That's right. Well, no, especially not you.'

I want to kill my own sister. I want to drown her, preferably in the Seine, like that guy tried to do with his kittens in The Age of Reason. Except that he failed miserably, and I wouldn't. Not loving her would help, I guess. Wonder if my murderous thoughts make me a fully-fledged existentialist – or a fake one. Who cares. Hate Sartre, anyway. And as for de Beauvoir. Seriously. Don't even get me started on that ugly old bird. Both of them, ugly. Regurgitating their own words again and again, sucking their cud dry. Disgusting. Surprised they were not born in Vukovar. Why did I even read those stupid books? Shame on me. Perhaps I could say to myself that I was young, I needed the money. Some sort of currency, anyway. A conversational ice-breaker, in days when I was trying to get in with the cool crowd. But, if I don't want to hang with people like Sartre and Boudoir (is how I like to call her), who is there left for me to hang around with. Cue the neon question mark, flashing alarm-red.

Lazar aside, is there anyone for me out there. Question. Bloody. Mark.

I spend the next two days in bed. Get up for a drink of water and a pee, then it's back to sleep again. No one bugs me, that's what I like about this family: everyone's too self-obsessed to seriously consider the wellbeing of another. Teodora diagnoses me anorexic at one point, and tries to get Mum to commit me to a clinic, but Mum tells her to go get herself a life. I have never heard my mum say anything so directional to anyone before in her life, and I develop a new sense of admiration for the woman who gave birth to me so reluctantly she broke my shoulder with her nut-cracking pelvis. I came here in pain. No wonder I find it hard to commit, to anything or anyone. Could my life get any sadder.

But then I wake up. I toss and I turn, I try and imagine I'm really sleepy, make sure the shutters are keeping out all the light, so my body's fooled into producing more melatonin, but the awful truth is I'm wide awake. And with no idea what to do next. I have visited this place before and didn't like it, not one little bit. It's called The Unbearable Lightness of Being, and Kundera has already written a book about it. Nice book. I actually burst into tears when Karenin died. Here lies Karenin. He gave birth to two rolls and a bee. Boo-hoo. In my defence, I was only ten when I first read the book. A mere cry-baby.

I push my forefinger under one of the slates on the shutters, the sunrays fight their way in. I let go. Back to the shadows. But not for long. I'm hungry.

I walk down the stairs, listening out for any signs of life. My cat, Miko, runs over to greet me. I pat my chest. 'Come, Miko, come!' He jumps up, I catch him and wrap him around my neck, like a warm collar of purr. Who needs a dog. We used to have a dog when I was a little girl. His name was Vuk, a wolf, despite the wolf being his mortal enemy back home, on the Macedonian Shar Mountain. I used to ride Vuk, until I got big and podgy. A passing, but nevertheless frightening phase. I was five, I was fat, and I started school which was full of little children. If that wasn't traumatic enough, Vuk took to collapsing on the ground the moment he saw me coming. I reckon I was deeply scarred by all of the above, but of course no one ever cared to notice. I had to learn how to sort my own self out. Just as well. Now I can make my own life decisions without relying on anyone else for help. Anyway, Vuk also grew up then grew old, and one day he bit this neighbourhood cunt who came to our gate to complain about his bark. Vuk only tried to protect us, but the judge ruled that he had to go, or die. Dad drove him, like, 400km south, but Vuk returned, what a good boy. Dad took him away again. He swore that he gave him to this friend who just happened to own a cherry orchard that needed guarding. A story later to be repeated with Rea, who of course was an actual wolf. Nowadays I stick to cats. I'm lucky to have Miko. He's probably the only person in the world Teodora has a healthy respect for. They never liked one another, and Miko used to stalk her like a prey, then pounce at her and scratch and bite until he's had his share of flesh. Oh how I laughed. Until one day Dad threatened to take Miko to the orchard, too, so I had to have a word with him, we had to think of another way for him to be. These days he only hisses at Teodora on a regular basis, and sometimes waits for her when she arrives home late, then pounces in front of her out of the darkness just to hear her scream. But he's keeping his teeth and his claws to himself, clever boy that he is.

'It's too hot,' I say. 'You need to get down.'

I can feel his paws fan out, releasing those deadly blades.

'Go on, Miko, have mercy. You must be even hotter than I am.'

He promptly retracts, and jumps onto the tiles.

'Good boy!' I open the fridge. 'Shall I see what I can find for a good boy to eat?'

He's grinning like a Cheshire cat. I take out some grapes, cheese and salami for me, and a piece of veal for him. There's lots of veal in that fridge. Wonder if my parents are expecting guests. Hope not.

After breakfast, I light a cigarette. I smoke it, light another. And another. When I cannot smoke no more, I walk into the street. It's almost midday. Everyone's inside, working, eating, screwing. I wander across the road and down the lane that leads into a derelict piece of no-man's land tucked out of sight behind a pretty row of houses. Dola. I like this place. I like derelict. Uncultivated. Too much tweaking confuses me.

School, people, books, food. Life in general. It can get too orderly. Left, right, backward, forwards. Which way again? It's like being lost in a labyrinth, but with no Ariadne to gift me with a ball of thread. So I resort to using a trapdoor option. Not that this is what I'm up to now, disappearing down the trapdoor. This time, I'm bona fide withdrawing from all social and anti-social activities. Okay, maybe this is a little like escaping via a very large trapdoor. With bells and ribbons on it. And a flashing No Entry sign.

Yeah. I reckon it's beyond my years wise of me to take the time off, gather myself up. See what's what. I couldn't do that in front of other people. I used to think the drink would help me get hold of my own bearings a little less painfully, but now I get a feeling that drink only makes things worse. Could do with a vodka right now, though, to help untie the knot in my chest that keeps tangling up all my good breath. Hope it's not cancer.

I light a cigarette. *Bijela Drina*. Very nice. Strong and straight, no aroma, no aftertaste. Just how I like it. The story goes the Sarajevo tobacco factory that makes it gets hold of the same tobacco Philip Morris uses for Marlboro, only a class below. Well I can't taste the fault, that's for sure. Only the merit.

I kick a few lumps of dry earth into dust, inspect the newly dumped rubbish on the heap. A rusty cooker. A washing machine without any buttons. Why would anyone keep the buttons. Another cooker, no oven door. A small fridge. An old woman. We stare at each other in blank surprise. I suspect she must be here to steal the rubbish and I wish I hadn't disturbed her. She must feel so embarrassed, the poor old witch.

'Good afternoon,' I say. I mean to sound reassuring, but instead I sound plain accusatory. How's that even possible. 'Nice day for it.'

She smiles, then beckons me with her jointy old forefinger. What is this, a murder mystery tour. I look back, but there's no one around, except for Miko, diving in and out of whispery long blades of scorched grass, riding high on the flesh of a baby cow. Good boy, keeping an eye on me like this. I glance at the old crone. Oh come on, Helena. She probably just needs help in handling the stolen good-for-nothings. A bore, sure, but hardly a threat.

It is almost interesting, okay, how amazingly unlucky I seem to be when it comes to old women in general. No matter what I do, or where I hide, they always seem to find me. Like for example Mrs Farkaš, this dilapidated neighbour of ours, who's forever appearing on her doorstep just as I happen to be sneaking by. She lives in one of those Austro-Hungarian houses made out of Danube mud, and certainly smelling like it. I guess I feel a little sorry for the silly old goose, living in such a dark and dingy place all by her lonesome, but still I try and avoid her as much as I can, and for good reason, too.

'Please! Please!' She whines, the moment she sees me coming down the path. 'I need urgent assistance!' I know she doesn't, this is but a ploy to get some company, or something equally sad, but I seem totally unable to muster enough courage to tell her to fuck off and die. Instead, I follow her inside and help with whatever imaginary task she happens to be struggling with on that day, like giving her antique gas fridge a gentle shove to make it snap back into life.

But not too gentle, or she goes, 'Come on, boy, work those muscles!'

Or too hard. 'If this is how you treat your girl, your brute, then I have nothing but contempt for you, and pity for her!'

Yeah, and for some reason she thinks I'm a boy. I did try and tell her otherwise when I was still young and naïve, and into wearing pretty dresses, but it only resulted in an additional twenty minutes of completely useless discussion. And still, as I'd finally manage to push my way back onto the street, her claw marks ridging all the way down my back, she'd take my hand and say something like, 'We make a good couple, don't we, my dearest Miron? You know I want to be your servant forever. Stop chasing skirts, come back to me, let us live as man and wife like we already are in the eyes of Our Father and his sweet Lord child, Jesus Christ.'

So yeah. She doesn't only think I'm a boy, she thinks I'm her straying husband who, if I had to hazard a guess, is probably long dead and gone. Nice one, old woman. Did a lot for my budding self-esteem at the time.

Back to my so-called present moment, I find myself following the rubbish thieving old woman through the wild patch of dwarf corn and over a hill built from all kind of rubble deposited here by the locals, and not so locals. I never liked going over that hill, not even when it was covered with snow and good for sledging. I suspected it of hiding corpses of long disposed of dogs and children, and I will continue to do so to my dying day. The sun is burning a hole in the back of my neck. I could really do with that vodka.

Through a young apple orchard, and a wooden gate we go, entering a garden filled with flowers and vegetables and fruit trees as old and gnarly as the old woman I'm traipsing after, then suddenly I realise: this is Baba Lepa!

I knew of her all my life. If I wouldn't sleep when I was little – and I bloody well wouldn't – my dad used to spend hours trying to soothe me with stories of great battles fought in the glorious history of the human race. My mum soon resorted to using a stick – oh she made for one very bad cop! – by telling me that if I didn't go to sleep, and pronto, Baba Lepa would fly over on her black goat with fiery eyes, and take me away to feed me to her hungry toads. Then she'd go outside and run an actual stick across the shutters, saying in a raspy echoey voice, 'Helena… Come to me, Helena… My babies are croaking hungry… Come, Helena, come and help me feed my babies…' Not very nice, was it, doing such a thing to an already plenty enough nervy child. I would freeze with fear, and dare not make a noise, or go to sleep, for the rest of the night. But the next evening I would kick off against the curfew all over again, go through the whole performance, regret it when the fear paralysed and pinned me to bed, until the next night that is. And the next. I'm not sure why I did it, or how long it lasted, but that's how I encountered Baba Lepa, so to speak, for the first time.

Baba Lepa lived in a big yellow house diagonally opposite from us. The shutters on the street side remained tightly shut for as long as I can remember; I never saw her leave or enter through the secure iron gates. Alone and invisible, we only knew she was there because of all the visitors that descended upon the place every single Sunday. They'd tuck their cars into every nook and cranny on and around my street, then wait patiently for their turn.

'She must be making a fortune,' Dad would say. 'What do you think, girls, maybe I should get your mum a crystal ball and a gypsy scarf, and she can earn us all some extra cash? Then we can all go to Paris, climb on the top of the Eiffel Tower and throw ice cream scoops at the gendarmes.'

'Yes!' I'd say. 'Go on, Mum! So we can go to Paris!'

Did I mention that I was one extremely gullible child.

'Maybe she really helps people,' Mum would say. 'Maybe she gives them hope.'

'Or maybe she robs them blind,' Dad would say. 'Hope included.'

'Come in, child,' says Baba Lepa. 'You'll burn to cinders in that sun.'

I step onto the red painted veranda. She points at the chair with flowery cushion. 'Make yourself at home. I'll just go and fetch some refreshments.'

I search inside myself for the usual feeling of unease, but I can't find any. Taken over by the sheer sense of awe, I expect. For never before in my life have I been anywhere near a place like this. Where do I even begin. Back in the garden I could swear I almost saw something. Don't ask me what. Guess it was something intriguing enough to catch the corner of my eye. But when I looked, actually turned around and looked, all I could see were raspberry bushes, and butterflies. As is the case with most houses around here, when you stop walking on the soft earth and start hitting the concrete, you know you've left the garden and entered the front yard. Ours was pretty straightforward, a paved path the car took to the garage, a place my sister and I used to play ball games, before I started disliking her as a person, and a place where I'd let Marijan slip his tongue down my throat and a finger up my knickers. Baba Lepa's front yard is another story entirely; another world, even. There are flowers everywhere, for starters. And I mean everywhere: in hanging pots, in sitting pots, in flower beds, in vases, glasses and also stuck into various bottlenecks. Up there amongst all the rose bushes and other flowers, no I wouldn't happen to know the name of, nest life-size sculptures of man and women embracing one another, kissing and, yes – frolicking, but not in a rude way. Just hanging together, passing the time of the day, I guess. At the back of the veranda, under a thick vine canopy, sits a huge wooden table with, I count, twelve chairs around it. Further down, there are a couple of brightly woven hammocks suspended in between three silky skinned cherry trees. I try to imagine Baba Lepa taking her afternoon nap in a hammock. Er – I don't think so. But if not her, then who. Moving swiftly on to the middle of the yard with rocking horses, ducks and I reckon pigs, roughly carved out of fat bits of tree trunk. I have seen children crossing the road so they wouldn't have to walk by Baba Lepa's house, and I have never seen no child entering that gate. Which, by the way, is painted in a thick black gloss on the outside, but a rich golden colour on the inside.

Well I am speechless, to say the least.

Baba Lepa comes back, holding the tray laden with goodies. I move to get up and help, she waves me back into my chair. 'Thank you, I can manage.'

A bowl of cherries, a jug of water with ice cubes, mint leaves and lemon slices summersaulting about, a few glasses – and a small bottle of bright red liquid. I know home-made cherry brandy when I see it. My triple exclamation mark favourite.

Baba Lepa laughs. 'Don't get too excited.' She pours a glass of water and puts the glass in front of me. 'Help yourself to cherries. But I will not be giving you alcohol. Alcohol is bad for people like you.'

Frankly, I'm feeling a fair bit disappointed, but what can I do. Old people are eccentric. I don't blame them, they must be sick and tired of always acting good and proper, and probably feel plain dumb for wasting their lives on being polite. Now they go, 'Fuck you world!' and no one dares blink an eyelid, except out of envy.

But: I'm not sure what she meant by people like me. Maybe she meant children from mixed marriages. Maybe she's as political and prejudiced as the most of the rest of this godforsaken town.

I reach for a cigarette, then hesitate and give Baba Lepa a questioning glance.

'You can smoke if you wish,' she says. 'Cigarettes won't be what moves you on.'

'Moves me on? Where to?'

Baba Lepa motions towards the sky. 'Up, up, and away.'

'You mean like death?'

'Exactly like death.'

Except that I know that exactly like is neither exactly, nor like. I wish people didn't speak in riddles. Time to change the subject. But what am I supposed to talk about with the ancient one? I point at the random sculpture of a couple. 'They look like they're having fun.'

'Most certainly!' She walks over and stands in between the marble people, gently patting their heads. 'These two here, Agape and Pankratios, they've been with me the longest. They do spend their time together in the most pleasant of ways!'

Okay then.

'Of course, Pankratios means all powerful.' She winks at me. 'Isn't Agape a lucky girl? Her name, by the way, it means love.'

Lazar once called me a lucky girl. Can't remember why, he must've been joking. All I know is I could do without these random flashbacks. I only met the man twice, and have far too much to think about already, don't need him crowding my head.

Baba Lepa moves on to a statue of a lonely looking girl. Her hair's long and fluid, but her body's startled, like she's just been shot.

'And this here is Helene.' Baba Lepa runs her hand down Helene's luscious locks. Her name means corposant, do you understand?'

'Holy body?'

'Good girl! Have a cherry.'

I take a cherry and eat it. What! This is the nicest thing I have ever put into my mouth and I want a recipe. 'But why is she so sad?'

'Well spotted.' I reward myself with another cherry. 'Ever since she was born, Helene felt that she was special. So special, in fact, she thought herself quite unlike the other girls and boys. Special, different and unique, Helene lived a very lonely life. Nothing ever seemed to happen to her. She saw good things happen to those around her, she saw them coping with the bad. Eventually, she started to long to be more like them, to experience a life more ordinary. So one day she decided to stop being special, different and unique, and become just like everyone else. But, as much as she tried, no matter how hard she forced herself to be like the others, Helene couldn't make herself out in their image. She could not be like them. Nor could she go back to being special, different and unique like she was before. And this is how we find her – stuck in between two impossible ways of being, both but a useless attempt to overrule her true destiny, as appointed to her by the powers of the unknown.'

'Sad,' I say. I would really like to polish off the cherries, but don't want to come across as greedy. Maybe I'll take one more, just make sure I don't pick the biggest one in the bowl.

There's something else.

A feeling.

In the centre of my forehead.

I feel...

...high.

Why do I feel high.

Baba Lepa weaves her way back onto the veranda. She is quite a mover, for a woman of, like, one hundred and ninety-three. 'You think it's sad?'

'Yes, I do. I think it must be very sad being her.'

'And how about being you?' Baba Lepa pulls a pack of cards out of her blue apron with white rabbits hopping all over the place, and hands them to me. 'Shuffle, if you would.'

'Oh no, I'm never sad,' I say. 'I'm not that pathetic.'

'Shuffle,' she says. I guess I may as well. A few cards fall out of the deck, and again. I'm not someone you'd call a splendid shuffler. Unlike Teodora. She's very good at it. All card games, in fact. I know she cheats, but damn I have no skill to prove it. 'Cut.'

Baba Lepa first has to show me how, and soon I cut like a pro. She collects the cards and starts laying them on the table in front of her. Not the crystal ball after all. She examines the cards for a long time, making small noises now and again.

I wait for the insight to come. And wait. After a while I start feeling sleepy. I notice four or five bees, buzzing from one flower to the next. Two cats, sleeping on each side of a giant terracotta pot with one of those cartoon cactuses towering above it. Sparrows chit and sparrows chat, flying around my head. The river is cool and green, I put my hand into it and it turns into glass. If I scream real loud, I will wake up all the lemons.

I open my eyes. The air is cooler, and dusky purple. I feel rested, and pleased to know where I am for once. As for Baba Lepa, well she's nowhere to be seen. The cards have also gone, so have the cherries. The table and other chairs, gone. I take this as my cue to leave. But not before I thank my hostess for having me. And arrange another visit – even a hermit like myself needs a friend to eat cherries and talk Greek mythology with.

'Excuse me…' I go, softly. I walk up to the door leading into the dark house interior. 'Excuse me?' I knock on the door frame. And louder. 'Excuse me?' I croak.

THE KINGDOM OF YUGOSLAVIA
Fourth Enemy Offensive
Battle of Neretva
March 1943.

'Hey! Wait up!'

The sound of heavy boots crunching through the snow can mean only one thing: my companion is still with me.

'Where have you disappeared off to?' Black Petar catches up, puffing like a small steam engine, or perhaps more aptly, a lazy fat man with his arteries clogged up with plaque and his heart encased in a lardy coffin.

'How about you try and keep up for once?' I say. 'You know, if you really must copycat, why not copy the behaviour of a healthy human?'

'Like who?'

Good question. 'A non-smoker would be an excellent start.'

Last decade Black Petar got himself addicted to smoking a daily box of fat black cigarillos that stank like a burning heap of dung beetles. The decade before, it was the brothels: first night in a new town, he would vanish without a trace, only to resurface a few days later, most often than not nursing a broken heart as well as diseased penis.

'The whole point of seeking out a prostitute,' I said. 'Is that you are not required to fall in love in order to have sex!'

'It is not up to me who I fall in love with, where or when!' he replied. 'Besides, human females are well known for their delicious irresistibility. I don't suppose you'd understand.'

And so it went on. As apprentices go, Black Petar left a lot to be desired.

We march on through this silent land. All the animals – the birds, the wolves, the brown bears – have moved to the lower ground, where the bodies of fallen soldiers offered a much welcome feast. It has been a long harsh winter. The mountain was ravenous.

Black Petar clears his throat. 'Been meaning to ask...' He looks at me, hoping for encouragement. I offer him none. 'I know you are not too fond of the fact that I'm a natural-born copycat – don't ask me how I know, I just do.'

'You certainly come blessed with many a talent.'

'Exactly! I mean – thank you!'

'What is your query?'

'Well, I've been thinking: I can't be that different from your other students. Otherwise you wouldn't have taken me on.'

'I do not choose my students. They are allocated to me.'

'Oh.' Black Petar falls silent. Alas, it does not last. 'I just had another thought! Do you remember that old witch who read my cards at Sarajevo fairground? It was the summer of 1923, just after I joined you? She told me I was born with a dramatic streak that must be expressed – or else! Perhaps I'm not a copycat, perhaps I'm just an actor!'

'She was not a real witch,' I say. 'If she were, she would have told you there is no such thing as a dramatic streak. Not for us, at least, what with drama belonging exclusively to the human domain.'

'Oh dear, oh dear, oh dear.' He acts worried. Except that Visitors have no use for worry, and hence no such a capacity. Black Petar does not seem to know this.

'I'm like that ugly little creature that changes its colour according to its environment, you know the one I mean? The frog-shaped one? But with a tail?'

'Chameleon?'

'Yes! Just like a chameleon, I seem to absorb the energy of my environment. Can't help it!' He drops on his knees right in front of me and puts his hands together as if in human prayer. Where did he learn to do this? 'Please, please know that I'm willing to learn from you, and I have nothing but respect towards everything you have taught me thus far.'

I step around him and continue to negotiate my way down the steep side of the mountain. Black needs to mimic the behaviour of human race stems not from his chameleon-like nature, or his so-called flair for dramatic arts, but from a very real condition called densing. Densing occurs when a Visitor, typically a young and inexperienced one, starts developing a yearning which goes beyond imitating purely physical behavioural patterns of a human. The energy of yearning, unique to the human race, is like no energy a Visitor has ever encountered: no matter how much warning we receive prior to our first assignment, most of us succumb to a phase of densing at some point during our time here on earth. To a human, yearning comes naturally – he is born, he yearns, he spends a lifetime trying to fulfil this yearning, he fails, and then he dies. For a Visitor to truly experience a yearning would mean relinquishing our original purpose, which is to move countless beings onto their next life. In order to do this, we need to remain as light and free as can be. Any attachment to material worlds, whether mental, emotional or spiritual, would only cause us to dense up and out of our purpose.

'Stop!' Black Petar grabs my arm. 'Over there!'

I free my arm and watch a young woman, dancing around the snow-covered clearing. She is strikingly beautiful, both by human and other, higher standards, with her long black hair gently cascading around her sweetheart face, her half-open eyes as deep and blue as the sea, her lips as red as–

'Butt-naked,' says Black Petar. 'Far too cold for that.'

'Black Petar,' I say.

'Yes?'

'Are you a fool?'

Black Petar thinks.

'Never mind,' I say. 'Looks like we have a job to do.'

'Yes,' he says. 'We must save the girl!'

'It is not our job to save her. Stay!'

I walk over to the girl. She must have been here for a while, for when I tread upon her clothes, half-buried in the snow, they are already frozen stiff. I scan her body. There is a red rash spreading from her chest down to her belly. I check her eyes from up close, they are looking but not seeing. Her skin is as pale as the snow she is dancing on, but her lips, ears and fingers have already turned blue. I arrive to a conclusion that the girl is delirious, most probably due to the combination of typhoid-induced fever and hypothermia – but not quite ready to be moved on.

'Doesn't she remind you of one of those sweet little porcelain dolls people like to keep on their shelves?' Black Petar joins me, even though I clearly instructed him to stay put. 'Let's just save her, eh? Come on, Baba Lepa! Look at her, she can't even see us, this means she's meant to live, not die!'

'We are not here to save anyone,' I say. 'We are only here to help them move on.'

'While I appreciate this may be how you feel about the situation,' he says. 'I, on the other hand, feel like I have no choice but to follow my conscience and retrieve this defenceless girl from the cruel clutches of untimely death.' He pauses. 'And it isn't only because she's pretty, young and naked. Those days are over!'

'If you lay a finger on that human,' I say, 'you will leave me no option but to report you to the elders.'

He turns around. 'What for?'

'Your evident desire to become human.'

'I never said I wanted to become human!'

'And yet your entire manner clearly indicates your desire to join their ranks.'

'Never!'

'You drink like them. You eat like them. You copulate like them. You wish to rescue and liberate – these are the unquestionable traits of a human being. A true Visitor would not dream of trying to modify fate, or manipulate life. A true Visitor would never forget that his only role here is to help a human being step over the threshold.'

'I know that! I am a true Visitor... I am! I just...' Black looks at the girl.

'I don't know, I guess I just want to help.'

'That is not wrong.' I force myself to place my hand upon his shoulder. 'Look, there is no shame in becoming human. I will ensure that you get the best densification enforcer this side of the Earth Moon. The process is quick and tolerable, pain-wise, and once you are a fully-fledged human being, you will have absolutely no recollection of your time as a Visitor, so you will be free to live and die as a completely ordinary human being.'

Black looks petrified. 'No! Please... I don't want to live like them! Or die! I absolutely don't want to die like them!'

I gaze off into the mid-distance, pretending to ponder his plea, but really watching the girl sway her hips and flutter her arms through the crystal-clear winter air; slower and slower her movement grows, entering that last, sleepy stage of hypothermia, the point of no return. 'Very well, Black Petar. Consider yourself on probation. But if you ever utter even one more syllable on the subject of your dramatic streak, or your chameleon nature, or your feelings in general,

I will not hesitate to drop you off at the nearest assembly site!'

'Thank you, Baba Lepa!' Black tries to kiss my hand, but I am quick to pull it out of his reach. 'I will never let you down again!'

The next moment, two men emerge from the woods on the opposite side of the clearing. As one, Black and I pull back into the mountain's shadows.

The first man bursts onto the clearing like a brown bear with a bee under his bonnet. Unusually tall, he is wrapped up in what appears to be lady's fur coat, fastened together with a red silk scarf. His head, on the other hand, seems unusually small, half-hidden underneath a high fur hat and an impenetrable looking unkindness of raven-coloured beard dangling off his hollow cheeks. The badge on his hat, kokarda, with the unmistakably byzantine two-headed eagle and a cross, identifies him as a member of the Chetnik Detachments of the Yugoslav Army – or Chetnik for short. His hands are wrapped in strips of soft leather, with only tips of his fingers exposed to the elements. He is carrying a large bare blade in his left hand; with his right, he is clutching onto a homemade walking stick made out of a straight piece of oak.

The other man scuttles on behind. He is smaller and altogether finer-featured than his friend, with the look and mannerism of an undernourished bat. This unfortunate impression is not helped by his attire of black uniform and a dark grey cape, fluttering in his nervous wake. He is carrying a rifle on each of his scrawny shoulders, and a string of hand grenades attached to a thick leather belt. His face looks mean, miserly, pinched by either nature or nurture into a tight expression of absence. On top of his head rests a felt cap, made out of the same material as the cape, with a metal badge in a shape of a highly stylised letter "U" sitting crookedly just off centre. "U" stands for Ustasha: he is as a member of the Croatian Revolutionary Movement. An odd pairing indeed. Because, besides their plight to drag their absent King back onto the Serbian throne, so that he could restore their beloved country to a more tangible state than a mere concept of the Greater Serbia, Chetniks' main claim to fame is their utter derision of all things Croat. And as for Croats, they tend to see their Serbian neighbours as rabid hounds from the Byzantine underworld, to be put down as swiftly and diligently as possible. I wonder what kind of fate has twisted these two opposites together.

I check on Black Petar, who appears perfectly centered and calm. Good. Whatever happens next is meant to happen. All we can do now is sit and wait for it to pass.

'Ivan? Do you see what I see?' The Chetnik rubs his eyes in a theatrical manner, before starting to circle around the girl, like a shark circles before it rushes in to grab its prey. The girl is now standing in the middle of the clearing, completely motionless and with her eyes closed. 'Check that pile of rags over there, see if you can find any clues.'

'Clues as to what, brother Vuk?'

'Clues as to this one's identity, you idiot! She could

be a spy. Or – I don't know, maybe one of those new weapons of mass destruction Archbishop Lang talked about after the Germans and Italians gave those Basque dogs in Guernica a damn good trashing.'

Ivan scratches his head. 'I do like listening to what you have to say, my brother Vuk, even though I don't understand half of it.'

'I don't need you to understand me, I need you to do as I tell you.' Vuk points at the girl's clothes. 'Check them out. And stop calling me your brother, I'd rather cut my own throat – and yours – than have a Croat as a brother.'

'That's funny, because other Ustashas, back in the garrison, used to say exactly the same thing, about wanting to cut Serbian throats, and what not,' says Ivan. 'Which I found confusing, seeing how we are all fighting for the same cause.'

'The same cause?' Vuk snorts. 'Is that what you think?'

'Yes,' says Ivan. 'A Serb and a Croat, fighting shoulder to shoulder so that one day we could all live together as one nation, and share the land of our forefathers.'

Vuk laughs. 'Funny little fucker, aren't you? Tell you what this war is all about: first we get rid of the Communists, then we get rid of the Croats – until the very last one is either dead or gone. No offence.'

'None taken,' says Ivan. 'On the contrary, I am thoroughly enjoying our little debates. The soldiers back at the camp barely ever spoke to me, you know.'

'You don't say.'

Ivan sighs. 'It's true. I used to sit in the circle

around the fire for a long time, and nobody would say a word. But the moment I left to do my errands, they would all start chatting and laughing and joking. At least that's how it seemed to me. Just as well I'm not a paranoid man.'

'No?' Says Vuk. 'So what made you cut those guys to shreds, then?'

Ivan shifts his weight from one foot to another, shrugs. 'All I know is that one of them snatched away my blanket, and wouldn't give it back. He then threw it to the young man who had joined the unit only a few days back, who whipped out his tinkle and started pissing all over it. I just saw red, and that's the last thing I remember, I swear to God.'

'I never saw a carnage quite like it,' says Vuk. 'It took four big men to drag you away from those bodies.'

'That sounds terrible… On a brighter note, if I didn't do what I did, and you didn't do what you did, you and I would probably have never met.'

'Which would've been a great shame indeed.'

'Glad you think so.' Ivan hesitates. 'So…What did you do to get yourself court-martialled?'

'Nothing.'

'Nothing?'

'That's right,' says Vuk. 'I'm an innocent man.'

'Innocent,' says Ivan. 'Right. I won't argue with that.'

'Wise decision.' Vuk walks up to the girl. 'How about you, eh? Do you wish to quarrel with me?' He holds a blade to her face. She remains stock-still. He presses the silver blade against the side of her neck until a thin trickle of blood starts making its way down her shoulder and the side of her breast, like a soft red velvet ribbon that might have fallen out of her hair whilst she was dancing a night away with her beloved. 'Just as I thought, no quarrel at all.'

'She is a partisan!' Ivan holds up a cap with a red star attached to it. 'Vuk! She's a partisan! What do you reckon this means, eh, do you reckon she's been sent here to ambush us?'

'I reckon no such thing.' Vuk throws down the fur coat and unbelts his trousers. 'I reckon she's no longer following anyone's orders... Just like you and me.' He manoeuvres the girl onto the coat, which is not an easy feat, considering her body must be almost frozen by now, uncommunicative.

Black Petar buries his head in his hands. Good boy. This is human business. Nothing to do with us.

'What,' starts Ivan. 'Vuk? Er – what is it you are proposing to do next? With that girl, I mean? Because, I say we leave her here, just as she is, and we turn around and walk in the opposite direction, pretend we've never even seen her. Is that a yes? Vuk? Come on, let's be on our way.'

'Shut up, you Ustasha wimp.' Vuk arranges himself on top of the girl, until his legs are firmly wedged in between hers. 'You'll get your turn.'

Ivan yelps, then turns away.

I watch on. Seen it all before, men pushing women underneath them, entering their bodies again and again until they have had enough, and afterwards either killing them, or letting them go, and other times still coming back for more. I do not think there is an exact pattern to this particular kind of violence, except that a man is almost always a perpetrator. Men are physically stronger than women, of course, but I suspect there is more to it than that. Over the last couple of thousands of years, I watched women collectively forcing themselves out of the safe confines of the matriarchal culture and into the highly dysfunctional patriarchal society. I have no idea why. Perhaps it was evolutionary tactics designed to either save a race, or bring it to its extinction. In any case, mass-rape conditioning seems to have played a very important part in this transition, and it continues to do so to this very day.

Back to the here and now, Vuk collapses on top of the girl and everything goes silent. Ivan remains still, his head hung low. Black is tracing the lines of his left palm with his right forefinger. The landscape pulsates with indifference.

I count the seconds, safe in the knowledge that every stillness is but a mere calm in between storms. And sure enough, I barely reach twenty, when the silence is pierced by a high-pitched shriek. Vuk drops off the girl, and rolls down the steep slope, until his body hits the very rock behind which Black Petar and I are hiding. Vuk's eyes readily await my gaze, and it is only when I spot the blood pouring out of the deep wound in his abdomen that I realise why.

'Save me!' he whispers. 'Please…'

I shake my head. Black Petar peers into Vuk's face. 'Good riddance!'

'Brother Vuk!' Ivan grabs the girl, who is now

standing bolt upright, still holding Vuk's dagger. 'What do you want me to do with her, do you want me to tie her up?'

'Kill the bitch.' As Vuk tries to laugh his mouth fills up with blood. 'Kill them all, kill every enemy of the sacred Serbian land, kill them all dead, brother Ivan!'

'Did you just call me brother, my brother Vuk?' Ivan glances towards Vuk, delighted, holding up a thumb. The next moment, the girl is on top of him, howling like a wounded animal, frantically hacking at his chest and face, before giving out one last blood-curdling cry and collapsing onto the soft red sludge next to Ivan's mauled body.

I leave Vuk with Black Petar and rush over to Ivan, who is still alive, and more than willing to move on. Thank God for small mercies, for we have wasted enough time on this mountain. I make my mark, then walk over to Black Petar, who is already crouching next to the girl. 'Dead?'

He nods.

'And Vuk?'

'He fought me to the bitter end.'

'Serbs are known to do that.' I look around this once pristine, snow-embraced place, now soaked with blood and littered with human remains. 'We must continue down to the river. The fallen are calling.'

MYTHICAL PROPORTIONS

'Where were you all day?' asks Mum.

What's up with the third degree. Even as a child, I came home when I got hungry, which I guess was often enough – the chubby little thing that I was – for her never having to worry about my so called whereabouts.

'I was sunbathing in Dola,' I say. 'Why?'

'You – sunbathing?' she says. 'Why do you have to be so difficult?'

What is she talking about. I'm so easy, I practically raised myself. I shrug, and walk off to the kitchen. May as well make myself something to eat, because that's how difficult I am. Dad is sitting at the table. Teodora to his left, holding his hand. Like a slimy limpet. To his right sits Lazar. I remember I'm wearing my old polka dot shorts and a vest covered in dirt and a cherry stains, and not even a smidgen of an eyeliner. Earth, please, please open up and swallow me. Oh, and there is a man sitting opposite Dad whom I don't even know. They all look, what's the word. Gravely concerned, or something.

'What's going on?'

Everyone looks up. I notice Lazar's real pleased to

see me for a moment, but then his eyes gloom over again. Seriously. Who died.

'Helena, dear!' Dad opens his spare arm, the one that isn't being mauled to death by Teodora. I walk over, dead cautious, unsure if I want to hug him in front of everyone. Also, whatever the hell is going on, I feel like I want to stay as I am with it, ignorant and oblivious, and touching my father will definitely make it real. He puts his arm around my waist and pulls me in. I feel as uncomfortable as can be. Then I notice there's a half-empty glass of red wine in front of him. So I empty it. By drinking it myself, that is.

'Helena!' goes my sister.

'He doesn't drink,' I say. 'Do you, Dad?'

'That's right, I absolutely do not. Hate the stuff.'

But he's obviously already had a glass or two, I can tell because he never says absolutely, nor does he ever hold me this close. I remove his arm, easy does it, and go sit in the empty chair next to Lazar, who seems the safest person around, plus he smells very delicious too. Teodora throws me a dagger. She must be in love with Lazar already, the slutty little whore that she is.

'So who died?' I ask. You see this in films, a person will enter a room and ask in a cheerful voice, So who died? and everyone will wag their eyes at them, because of course someone did actually die, which ain't no laughing matter, so shame on you, asker. Unfortunately, this is not a film, this is just another day in my so-called life.

Lazar clears his throat, says, 'Your father's colleague, your godfather I believe, Dragan Antić—'

Oh shit. 'Uncle Dragan?'

'I'm afraid he's gone,' says Lazar. 'Passed on.'

My beloved, happy-go-lucky, artistic godfather who always gave me money. For my birthday, for holidays, or if he just happened to run into me on the street – he'd always stop and give me a few banknotes. 'A girl's got to eat,' he'd say, and wink at me, but not in a pervy way, and ruffle my hair. People like him are not supposed to die.

'Passed on?' says Dad. 'They cut his throat, those Ustasha bastards!'

'Stevan… Don't do this to yourself. The police say it was a robbery gone wrong,' says the stranger. 'In any case, we know nothing for sure.'

'Wake up, Branko,' says Dad. 'It's time for all of us to wake the fuck up!'

Teodora starts to cry. Christ's sake! He was my godfather, hers is still walking about, that good for nothing, lazy, scaredy cat Uncle Mirko. I have never met a man so loathsome. All he ever does is eat, sleep, and tell rude jokes. Oh and criticise. Like godfather, like goddaughter.

'Why?' I ask. 'Why would anyone do such a thing?'

'Milicija are working on it,' says Branko. 'They promised to keep us informed of any new developments.'

'Who are you?' I ask.

The man smiles. 'My name is Branko. I work with your father.' He offers me his hand. Very nice hand, for an old guy. I like Branko already. Perhaps he could be my new godfather.

'They didn't like his poetry!' Dad booms in his lecturer voice. 'They were scared of his mighty verse!'

'Who's they?' I ask, not because I want to know. I'm not even sure why I ask. Just making some noise, I guess.

Dad looks at me as if I were stupid. Ouch. Bad Daddy. 'The Ustashas, my daughter. Ustashas. They've found their way back from the darkest corners of the Stygian crypt and now walk amongst the living seeking the death of their old enemy.'

Oh. That old chestnut, as very old people would say. Ustashas are Croats who hate Serbs, and Chetniks are Serbs who hate Croats. I don't think they do much else besides plotting each other's demise, not much of a raison d'être if you ask me, but I've witnessed worse.

'Do these guys even exist?' I ask. 'I thought they all died in the World War II, or moved to Australia.' I think for a moment. 'Or, like, Argentina.'

Teodora sniggers. Oh I'm so going to get her for that.

'If only,' says Branko.

I pour myself a glass of wine. Teodora looks at Dad straight away. He does nothing. I drink it, slower that I normally would, because:

a) I'm not actually allowed to drink alcohol, not since I came home one night so sloshed I actually peed my knickers right here in the middle of the kitchen floor, for all to see, and

b) I'm not too keen on Lazar thinking of me as a lush. Too many people already do. Why, I do not know. I drink just like anybody else. Except of course when compared to those who do not drink at all.

'If only! Too late for wishful thinking – they came

to his door, in the middle of the night, and they slit his throat on that doorstep, in front of his wife and child. You've read Nevenka's statement, you've seen the state she was in. Two of them held her back, one held their boy, and they made them watch. They laughed as they cut, she said, they held him down and they cut into him, and they laughed! Too late for wishful thinking...'

I wish I stayed at Baba Lepa's. It was safe and peaceful there.

Dad bangs his fist against the table, scares the shit out of Teodora. 'He went down like Kraljević Marko, may God bless his soul!'

Well, strictly speaking, Kraljević Marko, the greatest Serbian hero that has ever lived, was killed by no man. What really happened was that this fairy called Vila Ravijojla told him he was going to die, and so he went and died. Dad knows this. Or has he forgotten. I open my mouth to put things right, then change my mind and top up my glass instead. Lazar is looking at me. I try my hardest not to blush. I really fancy him. Despite the tragic circumstances surrounding our present encounter, I still hope I will end up shagging him, and the sooner this happens the better, because the world is spinning off its axis, and I am determined not to be the only secret virgin whirling through space for eternity and beyond.

Mum enters the kitchen. Looks like she's been crying. 'Why is Helena drinking?' She whips away my glass. 'We wouldn't want her to have another accident, would we now?'

'What's wrong with you?' I get to my feet with

such force my chair hits the ground. 'Why are you being so horrible to me?'

Mum turns around and slaps me across the face. We stand there. No one moves. No one says a word. Miko runs in, jumps up into my arms. He growls at Mum. 'You selfish girl,' she says. 'Take that scruffy beast out of my kitchen before I wring his neck.'

'Nice one, Mum!' I scream. My voice comes out all tin and no opener. Miko makes a noise that sounds like it's coming from the deepest darkest pockets of Hell. 'Go back to your imaginary world, why don't you!'

And with that not even remotely witty putdown, I march out of the kitchen. Once I'm on the stairs, the tears start coming down thick, fat and fast. I get into my room, but I don't feel safe. Perhaps that's how it's going to be from now on, I will never feel safe again, anywhere. My own mother is a violent, evil being who doesn't like me, has never loved me and is suddenly hell-bent on destroying me. At least now I know who Teodora has taken after. Can't believe she did it, can't believe she physically attacked me in front of everyone. In front of Lazar. Fucking giant exclamation mark. Well that would be that, shagging wise. How can anyone fancy a beaten up child. Well – anyone who isn't a pervert. I want to die with shame, and I want to take a few people with me.

COMPANY WE KEEP

I make a beeline for Marylyn, no shoes, no money, no nothing. Lucky for me, Aleks is already propping the bar, looking lonely and therefore surely in the mood to keep a fellow Vukovar reject in booze and cigarettes for the evening.

Aleks greets me as a long-lost friend, which will do for now.

'Grab a table,' he tells me. 'And I'll grab us a beer.'

'And a double vodka!' Hate beer. Hate all alcohol, in fact. That's why I'm always chewing gum. To disguise the taste of alcohol. And cigarettes. Don't like the taste of them, either. But vodka's alright, I just pretend I'm drinking water.

Aleks returns bearing gifts. 'So, how are you doing, you dark horse? Or rather, who are you doing?' His eyes look like pee holes in the snow. How come I never noticed this before. 'Faster, pussycat! Spill! Spill! It's been way too long since you last confession.'

Ew. Although Aleks claims to be my friend, as well as a fellow lost soul, I don't actually like him. And I certainly don't trust him. Not sure why – reckon he could be lacking in, what's that word again. Oh yes –

integrity. He likes to know stuff about other people too much, and prides himself on being a walking gossip database. But I have to give him something. He's financing this evening's oblivion trip, after all. 'Where do I start?' I down the vodka. 'My fucking sister, honestly, if I stayed in that house I would've killed her.'

'Oh yeah? What's the little bitch up to now?'

And who are you calling bitch, bitch. It's not that I mind throwing Theodora to the wolves, it's just that Aleks is hardly a wolf, more like a badger crossed with slug. In any case, I suddenly no longer feel like making up stuff about my hateful sister. Instead, I go, 'Well, it's her friend, the red-haired girl, what's her name?'

'Tatjana?' says Aleks. 'The one with the huge jugs?'

'Yeah…' Jugs? Okay. 'Well, funny you should mention it, because she's just been diagnosed with adolescent carcinoma.' Here I make the expected pregnant pause. Yawn. 'And it's terminal.'

Aleks covers his mouth with both hands, the fat little fairy that he is. 'Which one?'

'Which one what?'

He takes an overexcited mouthful of beer, his little hands still shaking with anticipation. 'Which jug?'

'Both,' I say. 'The cancer's eating away at them. Pay attention the next time you see her. Her jugs – gone. More like espresso cups now.'

He nods. 'I will. Discreetly, of course.'

Alex and discreet is like Hitler and Hanukkah. Just can't be done. 'So yeah, Teodora's now jumping on the band wagon,' I prattle on. 'It's all about her, as per usual. Crying, cursing cruel fate, and being a general pain in the ass.'

'What's new?'

I take this was as a rhetorical question.

Quick rewind: after my mum smacked me one in front of Lazar, I ran to my room and threw myself into my bed, hoping to return to the place of blessed oblivion I seemed to have fallen into effortlessly in the not so distant past. But try as I may, it wouldn't come. Perhaps the past just wasn't distant enough. Miko wasn't helping either, attacking my toes and my hair, or whichever part of my body happened to poke out of the covers. 'Settle down,' I said. But he wouldn't. 'Settle down, you beast!' But he laughed at me, then bit the forefinger I wagged at him. Playfully, though. He's my friend, he'd never hurt me. Probably the only person in the world I could trust right now. Still, he had to go, because he was starting to go berserk, just like an overexcited toddler, or something. So I chucked him out, dived back under my sheets, sweated around a bit. Not that I sweat – apart from an occasional attack of cold sweats. Not even in the midst of the drippy Danube summer. Faulkner's South had nothing on Slavonija, this sizzling, immovable feast of ennui. Next, my skin started to itch. All over. Like I suddenly became allergic to something, or most probably everything.

Someone knocked on the door.

'Go away!'

Must sleep, must sleep, must sleep. I kept trying to hypnotise myself, but it simply wouldn't work.

Nothing worked. I sat up in bed and looked through the skylight, hoping for stormy clouds. But no such luck, the sky was still depressingly bright, cloudless and blue.

"Maybe this is the right moment to start writing my novel," I thought.

I sat at the dressing table, my parents being too mean to provide me with the walnut writing desk I wanted ever since my last birthday. Which was about three weeks ago. How was I supposed to become an internationally renowned novelist if I didn't even have a proper desk to write on. Some people write on computers and stuff. Lucky people, like those who were born in the West. Or belong to a much more forwardly developed family unit. Unlike moi.

I wished I spoke French.

I wished there was a storm.

I wished I lived in London.

I wished Uncle Dragan was still alive.

I wish people weren't such stupid bastards.

I sat at the table, paper a-ready. Ten minutes went by. I wrote, "In this place of song and happy memories, it is impossible to hide one's murderous intentions." But I didn't know how to continue, I wasn't sure what I was trying to say here, or even if it was me who was saying it. Which was the last drop. I slapped on some unscented talcum powder under my armpits, then poured some on my hair and shook it all off. My hand hesitated over the bottle of Armani Classic, the only perfume I'd ever wear. I heard they discontinued it, so I was having to stop myself from bathing in it. The Stone Women who sat outside their houses would wave their burning bulrushes at double speed as I walked by, smelling divine. They probably thought I smelt like a Devil's spawn, but I didn't care. I smiled at the thought, and sprayed on the perfume, not as much as I'd like, but still far more than necessary. Don't think I get that word, *necessary*. What's that. Kill me now.

Once outside, I immediately felt better. The Stone Women, the old women from my neighbourhood, were already out, perched on the wooden stools and benches, bulrushes smoking away the river mosquitos. Argh, the mosquitos were right bastards this year. Thank fuck Armani seems to repel them, wonder if that was intentional. I noticed that Lazar's car was still parked on the front lawn. But what do I care. I'm off to town. I'm off to have a good time. I'm not going to wait around for no old guy to come and find me already.

Aleks on beer is the most boring combination ever. Sloshing, slushing, slurring mess. Yet still he wants to gossip. 'Tell me about Iva, I hear she's like really involved with the you know what.'

I look around Marylyn, the only place in this backward town I'd be seen dead in. Midweek, and it's heaving with people. What's everyone celebrating then. I see a couple of familiar faces. I mean, they are all familiar, like it must be the case with all true hillbilly corners of this world, but at least the faces in here don't make me want to throw up on sight. 'The you know what?'

Aleks laughs like a fat Madonna. The Ciccone version, circa 1986.

He shakes his head. 'Now, now… No need to be coy. Politics is the new black. No one wants to be seen as being apolitical any more, darling. Heroin is no longer passé.'

'Huh?'

'Heroin, baby. Politics – opium for the masses? Hello?' He leans over and knocks on my forehead. I recoil in horror. 'Anyone home?'

'It was *religion*, you Marx-misquoting fool,' I say. 'And what the fuck's up with the knocking?'

Aleks makes a sad face. Like a fat melting clown. Triple ew. 'You got me sussed, girl. I seem to have displaced some of my vogue. Ya. Whatyagonnado.' He leans his head against the steamed-up window and closes his eyes. My cue to leave.

But before I do. 'Aleks? Are you saying Iva's involved with politics?'

He opens one of his serpent-green eyes, pins them down on me. 'Try up to her watery eyeballs. The Croatian Democratic Union party, the Ustasha lot. And their boss, Franjo Tudjman, ever heard of him? The One Who Won't Rest until the last Serb is either dead or expelled from Croatia? Preferably the former.'

'What's Iva got to do with it?'

'She's embracing the sins of her father, right, the big shot policeman, long-time supporter of Croatian independence, VIP CDU member, war mongering for the Croatian masses. Your friend Iva's becoming one of the most prominent representatives of Tudjman-jugend, and fast. Welcome to the Nazidome.'

'You're making this up!'

'Oh am I?' Aleks shrugs. 'Let's just wait and see what happens next, shall we? Because I also heard they have already started to skim off the top of the Serbian crème. Hope your beloved daddy is well tucked up in his bed tonight, with a gun under his pillow.'

I stare at him. 'What are you talking about, Aleks?'

He gives me a tired look. Not beer-tired, just tired tired. 'I am only trying to warn you, you oblivious little cunt.'

I'm standing in the corner, all by my lonesome. Aleks has left the building, in one of his typically self-induced huffs. Just as well. Except that now I seem to have run out of luck. Nobody wants to share with me, not even a fag. They say that whatever you're feeling carries through your energetic body into the ether. No wonder people prefer to keep their distance when you feel like shit. Nobody wants to sit around your stink. They have plenty of their own to go through I suspect. Fuck I'm tired. I'm also horny. I look around. Ew and ew. Or am I being too choosy. Is there such a thing.

Whoa. I think I may be a little pissed. Forgot to say I did manage to get a few large vodkas and a half a pack of Marlboros off this loser who couldn't believe his luck when I came over and said, 'Hey, you, go buy me a vodka, make it quick, and make it a double!' He tried to keep up for a while, then went to the loo and never came back. Found him passed out in the courtyard. I had to lurk forever, wait for these two fat slags to take turns in checking each other's beehive for fleas no doubt, but the loser's wallet proved to be a scoop of, like, a century. Was going to leave him some breakfast money, sure, but then I fucking looked in again, saw this little photo of an even littler girl, big mistake, because now I couldn't just take the money, not even one banknote, so I shoved the wallet back into his jacket pocket, then thought about it and pushed it deep underneath the layers of his clothes right next to his heart, think I might've brushed my fingers against his loser skin in the process, seriously didn't need that memory to haunt me to my dying day.

So this is the whole reason I'm standing here alone, minding my own business cause there's no one willing to share theirs with me. Or have I spoken too soon. Because in comes Iva, and I'm all ready to forgive and forget, when I spot she's hanging off the unnaturally log arm belonging to Vladimir, the Osijek-sleepover guy.

I move back into the shadows. Plenty of those in Marylyn, that's for sure. Iva waltzes around the joint, peers into booths, as if she's looking for someone. Fuck! She's probably on a search & destroy mission, eliminating the Serbian Intelligentsia as she finds them. That bitch! If I had a walkie-talkie, I could've warned my dad. Now I have to go all the way home to warn him, although frankly I think:

a) the night is still too young, and

b) Iva didn't seem that blood-thirsty anyway.

Plus, with the name like Ferlan, people start scratching their heads. Is it German? Is it Croatian? Is it a plant? Is it a mineral? One thing Ferlan doesn't sound is Serbian. Anyway. When Iva eventually leaves, it's safe to breathe again. And mingle. Except the last thing I'd want to do right now is mingle.

Truth is, I miss Iva. I seriously don't make sense even to my own self sometimes. The world is full of morons, and whatever else Iva may be, she isn't a moron. I feel like running after her. At the same time, I feel like I need Iva's – not to mention Vladimir's – company like a bullet in my head. Which reminds me, the other night I had a dream I was looking after this little girl, and she was playing with a gun that didn't look like a gun, as often happens in the dreamworld, so she went and shot herself right in her tailbone, didn't she. It was a horrid injury, the bullet got stuck near the back of her spine, the entry wound all gaping black and blue, I couldn't even look. I was supposed to help her, but I didn't. I didn't want to take the responsibility, I guess I convinced myself the wound would self-heal by the morning. It didn't. Anyway, it was a horrible dream, and what the fuck does it mean. Bet Freud would have a ball with it, except I wouldn't let him. Jung, on the other hand, I would.

Crap. I think I'm sobering up, and that just won't do. I look around, loath to make an effort. Should've kept that guy's wallet, fuck the little girl, she's probably dead anyway, shot herself in the back and bled to death. Arghh. This is my least favourite of all the miserable ways to be, this listless restless fucking state with no light coming through from either ends of the tunnel, so I have no choice but to stay in the middle, like a sitting duck, waiting for a train to hit. I don't want to be here, yet there is no place I'd rather be, now that just about sums up the recurring phase I keep going through, and it feels so bad so scary I would not wish it upon my worst enemies. Only joking – I actually would.

'*Guten Abend*, my little flower, *wie ghet's dir*?'

'Jovan!' Now this is the way to cheer me up, God, and a sure proof of your existence. 'How lovely it is to see you!'

Jovan kisses me on the lips, tries to push in his tongue, I spit it out, politely. '*Kuss mich jetzt!*'

'What's with the German?'

'*Ich bin ein Berliner*,' he says, then pulls a bottle of vodka out of his coat pocket – coat? in June? – and passes it to me. '*Prost!*'

Marvellous. I take a sip. More of a glug, really. Then another. 'Seriously though, why have you gone all *sprechensiedeutsch*?'

'Because I'm off to Germania.' He jumps on top of a neighbouring table, sends the stuff flying all over the joint. 'I'm out of here, mother fuckers, I'm out of this shithole, and I ain't never coming back, you small town suckers!'

'Get the fuck off!' goes the crowd. 'Get off, you asshole!'

'My asshole?' Jovan says. 'You want to see my asshole?' He starts undoing his belt and fiddling with the buttons. 'Why the hell didn't you say so? No need to be shy, we're all friends here…'

No fucking way I'm going to allow for this to happen, Jovan is the only friend I have left, not counting Miko, and I'm not going let his ass become a talk of the town. 'Get off! Jovan? Please! Get off!'

'Do as she tells you,' someone yells from the opposite booth across. 'We'd rather see hers, any time!'

Jovan stops undoing his trousers, hangs his head low and goes dead still, like he's playing statues. I sense trouble that is probably beyond even my comprehension.

'Oi! Get them off,' a group of sluts shout out. 'Tease, or die!'

The next moment, Jovan's crouching on the table in the booth across. I never even saw him fly. His head slowly turns from left to right and back again, like a cyborg, scanning in the faces, computing their fears. 'You, and you...' He points at the two women in the booth. 'Vamoose.' The girls climb out of the booth as if it were a pit that has suddenly come alive with snakes. The four remaining men throw a longing glance after them. Wish you were here, not me sort of a glance. 'Which one of you cowboys here expressed such burning desire to see my girlfriend's ass?'

Just for the record: I'm not his girlfriend.

The men stare at their hands, feet, whatever. Until one of them goes, 'Look, man, we have no beef—'

'Oi oi oi, think we got a winner!' Jovan grabs the man's arm and lifts it into the air. 'Helena! Over here, *Schatzi*.'

I don't wish to oblige, but the crowd sort of hands me over to him. I don't like this, any of this. I think I'd like to go home now. I take another glug of vodka. Perhaps this is all very nice, and fun, really, but the problem lies with me. Perhaps I'm just too fucking sober. 'Good girl, *ja*.' He takes an empty beer bottle and puts it to my mouth like a mike. Did I mention the music's gone dead like five minutes ago and everyone's crowded over, as thick as thieves and twice as ugly. Glug. 'Helena, please tell these good people, please inform them all just how degraded, how cheap it made you feel when this man here — ' he points at the man whose arm he's still aiming skyward. The man opens his mouth. 'I wouldn't speak if I were you, not without my lawyer present.' Did I mention that Jovan is a fully fledged barrister, or at least he was until he went all disillusioned, and, well, quite mad. Yeah. He was a proper genius, or shall I say, ein wunderkind, but then short circuited and kind of died. But not before he had almost bit a judge's finger clean off. Don't ask. 'When this man here called out for you to strip off and show him your cunt – how did it make you feel?' Right. That's it. I push against the wall of people. It pushes back against me. 'No words! This poor girl, she's so traumatised, she has no words to express the pain this man caused her by his indecent, no – filthy, proposal. Scarred for life. Ladies and gentleman! We must demand that justice returns to this world we're living in, let's drag it back from banishment the only way that really counts: an eye for an eye, a tooth for a tooth, and a scar for a scar!' He smashes the beer bottle against a corner of the table. The glass flies everywhere, people shift to save their skin. I grab the opportunity to squeeze through. 'Helena,' Jovan calls. 'Helena!'

But I'm out of there. Out of the hellhole, but where to now. Back to being a hermit, I guess. Back to where I came from. Back to where I don't belong. Oh God.

I'm freaking out here. I'm freaking right out. My body starts to shake, inside-out, and I need to run for cover, I need to be some place good and safe, but there's no place like home for me, there's no place like home.

LIEBESGESCHICHTE

'Helena! Wake up, babe! Helena!'

I open my eyes. All I see is darkness. Then a shape emerges, a familiar shape of something I hate. For some reason. Can't think why right this moment. Can't think. Can only hate.

'Fuck off, you moron.'

'I deserve it,' says Jovan. 'I truly do. I'm sorry. Took it too far, granted, but I was never going to cut that faggot. Rumble in the jungle, babe, is all that was.'

'I hate you.'

'Unwise,' he says. 'Because I'm the only person about who never gave up on you I searched and searched until I found you. Here. Asleep in the doorway. Classy.'

'Oh yeah? Who else was looking for me?'

'Nobody. Who do you think you are? A Holy Grail?' He helps me up. My legs are actually shaking. 'Can you walk? Jesus!' He lifts me up and swings me over his shoulder. 'Here we go. Nice and easy. *Gutten abend. Entschuldigung.* You're as light as a feather. *Bitte.* Just as well. *Auf Wiedersehen.* Off we pop.'

I come around into more darkness. 'Miko? Pspssss!' I call out for him, but he must've stayed out last night. I stretch. The movement brings up a strange scent, and at the same time a familiar one. I get a feeling something isn't right here. Sure enough, my bedroom door swings open on the wrong side of the room, and in comes Jovan, whistling a happy tune. And he's butt naked.

'Gutten morgen, mine Schatzi!' He throws open the shutters, the sun pours in like a golden shower, blinds me dead.

'Hey!'

'Sunshine's our friend,' he says. 'It helps our bodies produce vitamin D. Keeps the depression away. Makes our skin glow... Mmmmm!' He throws himself onto the bed next to me, and pulls me on top of him.

This man is a morning person. God how I hate those. 'What are you doing, let go!' Jovan looks surprised, but does as I say. What the fuck. I pull away, then notice I'm also butt naked. And, oh no, oh no, please God no, I think I'm bleeding. I pull the sheets around me and withdraw to the far corner of the bed. 'Helena? What's wrong?'

I start to cry. I don't know why. I cry and I cry. It's almost as if it wasn't me who was crying, but somebody else. Some stranger, crying her eyes out over nothing. Everything. Jovan comes over, tries to hold me. I won't let him. Then I do let him. He's saying nothing, so that's alright. The worst thing would be if he was all over me, saying stuff like, 'It's okay, baby, you cry if you want to.' As if I needed anyone's fucking permission. People always seem to be asking permission from others, "Permission to speak!", or "Permission to use the bathroom!", or "Permission to be myself, even if it kills me, even if it kills you!" Well fuck off, I don't need your permission, you're nothing compared to me, anyway, because I'm a superhero and this here is a superhero's party and so I'll cry if I want to.

Eventually, the stranger stops crying, leaves me with a headache. It's awkward now, because I obviously came on during the night, all over Jovan's sheets, and will have to address this sooner or later. 'I think I got my period, I'm sorry I messed up your bed.'

He puts his hands on my shoulders and looks at me, for a long while. I feel myself blushing, feel like he can see everything about me, even the stuff I myself cannot. Bet he made for one awesome barrister. 'It's okay,' he says, eventually, then lets go of my shoulders and lights two cigarettes. Gauloises. Stylish. 'It was a crazy night, right?'

I nod. Changing the subject. Smooth. 'You went all cyber Phantom, never saw you act like that.'

'Phantom's enough all by himself. He has no need for no cyber part.'

I consider. 'Suppose you're right.'

'The Ghost Who Walks.'

'Guardian of the Eastern Dark.'

'Yeah,' he says. 'I can do Phantom, easy.'

We smoke in silence. Then he turns to me. 'Helena, what do you remember from last night?'

'Marylyn. Aleks. Beers. Leaving Aleks behind.

Vodka. Some loser. You. Vodka. Leaving you behind. Walking home. You.'

'And afterwards?'

'I don't know, sleep?'

I can sense he's upset. What's up with that. 'Have you lost track of time like this before?'

'All the time.'

'Well that's just *eine kleine nachtmusik* to my ears.'

I put the cigarette out into a neighbouring house plant. 'Everyone does it, drinks too much, goes a bit hazy…'

'No, Helena, not everyone. And not all the time. And not at the age of – how old are you? Eighteen?'

'Yep,' I lie.

'Thank God for that.' He gives me another strange look. 'Because, you see: we slept together, you and I. Last night. I knew you'd had a drink, we both had, but I'd no idea how much. I mean, you seemed, well – interested. And most certainly awake.' Jovan puts his hand on my knee. 'I had no idea you were a virgin.'

'Shut up!' I push away his smelly hand. 'Of course I was awake! And not a virgin!'

'There's nothing wrong with being a—'

'I have told you, I am NOT a virgin,' I shout. 'So shut up, don't talk, *nicht sprechensie*, okay?'

'Not okay, young lady!' He gets to his feet, all serious and kind of old. How old is Jovan really? Lazar's age? What's with me and all the old guys anyway? 'I have behaved appallingly, and can hardly use the ignorance as a mitigating circumstance. One should never, ever, fuck young ladies under the influence of alcohol, no matter how hot they are, no matter if they're begging for it!'

'Was I begging?'

'No. You were not begging. You didn't have to.' He runs his fingers through his hair, pushes the shutters back a bit. Finally. There was enough heat in this room without the sun adding its twopence worth. 'I like you, I always have. I just want to get something straight, okay, so listen up: yes, I do fancy the pants off you, but I also find you funny, and cool, and altogether a great person to hang and while away time with.'

'Fine,' I say. 'But why all the fuss? What's done is done. Just don't tell anyone I was a virgin, okay?'

'Tell? Who do you take me for? Come here.' He stands in front of me with outstretched hand. 'Come.'

'No.'

'Come, come, pussycat, I have something for you.'

Silly Jovan. I laugh. 'You are being weird.'

'No? Okay.' He goes down on one knee. 'Helena, um, what's your last name?'

'Ferlan.'

'Helena Ferlan,' he goes. 'Would you marry me?'

We stare at each other.

'Of course not,' I say. 'What's wrong with you?'

'Nothing's wrong with me. I like you. So I want to marry you.'

'Because we slept together?'

'Well, that too. You could've been saving yourself for your husband, for all I cared. I never asked, just barged in, helped myself. But I do care, I want you to know this.'

'Is it because you're feeling guilty?'

'No. Yes. I don't know.' Jovan brushes his hand across my collarbone. 'The point is, why the fuck not?'

I feel all tingly. Especially in between my legs. 'I don't know. Maybe because we're not in love with one another?'

'I could fall in love with you,' he says. 'In fact, I may already have.'

'Was I that good?'

'What?' Jovan tries to hide a smile. 'Yeah, it was good. But not the point.' He looks me straight in the eye. 'Go on, let's have ourselves a party, then bugger of to Germany together. Start afresh, have fun, eat bratwurst, have babies—'

'I'll never have babies.'

'No babies is fine with me. So is that a yes?'

'Where in Germany?'

'Berlin, baby. Where only the edgiest would do.'

'Berlin's for artists.'

'Oh yeah? We'll fit in just nicely then.'

Me and Jovan in Berlin. Leaving Vukovar behind. Forever. A brand new start. A new language, a new way of expression. Freedom to be. Freedom to be an artist, a novelist, without having to suck off every dick along the socialist climbing ladder to success. Living in an attic filled with sky. Wearing head to toe black without people throwing garlic bulbs at you. New friends. Better friends. Better lovers. I'm sure Jovan doesn't really mean for us to be together together.

No more Vukovar.

Then again, I have not only read, but also watched Berlin Alexanderplatz, and I can still taste the wretchedness. Seriously, how come my parents have let me dip my fragile young psyche into the moral tar cooked up by such serious fuckups like Döblin and Bukowski and Miller.

'Ham on Rye?' My dad once said. 'Superbly funny.'

Well I can tell you something for nothing, it was not the funny bits that have stuck.

'Come to me.' Jovan is watching me like a hawk. 'Go on, you can do it. A few inches forward... Two steps to the left... No, the other left... See? Easy.'

I smile. 'I won't marry you.'

'Oh go on.'

I laugh. 'No.'

'But come with me still you will?'

'No.'

'Why?'

'I'll just run away again.'

He goes silent.

'I'll tell you what,' I say. 'What happened last night, I'd like to find out more about that.'

'Okay,' he says. 'Wow this is awkward – it's usually men who can't remember. You really are a bit of a hooligan, young Helena.' He pats my head, like it was a cat. 'Ask away, see if I can enlighten you.'

'You said: it was good.'

'Well it was. I have never—'

He breaks off.

'What, exactly, was so good about it?'

'It was hot. Both of us. We were hot.'

'You need to give me more details. Else I'm gonna

jump to a conclusion you can't remember it either.'

He scratches his head. 'How am I supposed to explain the feeling to a girl whose first sexual experience proved to be so remarkably forgettable?'

'Perhaps,' I say. 'You could show me.'

He looks taken aback.

'Sorry,' I say. 'Bad idea.'

'No! Not bad, just... Unexpected.'

I smile. My heart is beating so hard I can hear very little besides. Okay. What's done is done. I let the sheets fall onto the floorboards. What happens now.

LAST CHANCE SALOON

I am sitting on the floor of the corner of my bedroom, sobbing. I've been at it hard for almost half an hour: the tears are practically squirting out of the corners of my eyes, cartoon-style and never-ending.

Tears on tap. This happens to me sometimes. I'm never sure what causes it. The meltdown. In fact, I'm usually having an okay time before the tragedy strikes. Completely out of the blue, then wham – I'm back in my grief corner, overwhelmed, naked and crying my eyes out. There's nothing else left for me to do, but cry. Wait for the feeling to pass.

Jovan hasn't stopped ringing since we parted company three days ago. I take his calls, tell him to cool it. Tell him to fuck off. Well if I'm clinically depressed, then he must be clinically mad.

Yesterday:

'Daddy,' I said. 'I think I'm depressed. Like, really depressed. Clinically.'

Dad put down his fork. I felt a bit bad, spoiling his enjoyment of an apple pie like this. It's his firm favourite. And mine. 'What makes you think you're depressed?'

I shrugged. 'I don't know. It's just this feeling I have.'

'What kind of feeling, my love? Can you try and describe it for me?'

Why did he have to be so annoying. Why couldn't he just take my word for it. But I remained patient with him. And nice. 'No, Daddy, I don't think I can describe it. That's why it is called a feeling. Not a fact.' I could tell he wanted to laugh. I could just tell. 'Please don't laugh at me. I'm very upset. Now you're making me even more upset.'

He pretended to pat his stupid moustache with a napkin. Hiding a smile, I bet. I realised a while back he was quite an immature man. My father was childish. Shock horror. But also the truth. I mean, just look at his so-called moustache. Exactly. What moustache. Professor or not, he didn't have much of an idea about life. Or about how to take care of his facial hair, or his daughter's emotional health. Seriously. How did I end up this knowing and wise remains a mystery, practically a miracle.

'I can see you're upset. I am very sorry about that. But I feel we need to establish the real nature of your malady, before we call in the big guns.'

'The big guns?'

'Yes,' he said, looking dead straight, pretty grave even. 'Namely my friend Ludovik. Do you remember Uncle Ludovik?'

'The one with piercing blue eyes?' I picked up his fork and started to pick on his apple pie. 'Yes. Why?'

'He's one of the most influential clinical psychiatrists in Europe.'

'Why would you call him in?'

'Clinical depression is a very serious matter.'

'Are you pulling my leg?'

'Not at all.' I searched his face, but could not detect any traces of jest. 'If you're in trouble, Ludovik would be able to help. He's had decades of experience.'

'You mean with crazy people?'

'No, not crazy,' said Dad. 'He calls them PPs: psychologically provoked. Ludovik believes these people get stuck in a conflict that arises directly from exposure to an environment they find particularly challenging. If this conflict doesn't get resolved quickly, perhaps through lack of power or opportunity, it often gets internalised. I imagine this would be like eating a poisoned apple.'

Now I'm doubly worried. 'You know, Daddy, maybe I was mistaken. To use the word clinical, I mean. Maybe it's just my hormones.'

'I see.' He picked up his fork again. I started to edge towards the door. 'But, and just out of interest, what made you think you were depressed, clinically or not?'

'Oh,' I said. 'It's just that I haven't been out for days...'

'I thought I saw you spend all day Sunday curled up with a book on that deckchair under the old quince?'

'You did, but what I meant to say is that I haven't been out out, you know – no parties, no disco, no fooling around...'

'Well,' he said. 'Perhaps you're old enough to leave all that behind, and get on with the rest of your life. How's school?'

'It's still standing.' Too old to party? At sixteen? 'And I cried for hours the other day. Couldn't stop.'

'That's probably just alcohol, leaving your system.' He peered at me over his glasses, but his eyes were smiling. 'It's a well-known depressant, best stay clear.'

'I will, Daddy,' I lied. 'I definitely will.'

Then I went back to my room, took off my clothes, sat in the corner, laid my head on my knees and started to cry.

'I am not going to lie for you any more, Helena,' says Mum. 'Next time he comes, you tell him you're out. Such a lovely young man, too.'

This is the third time Jovan came around. I am starting to get a bit annoyed.

I'm also tempted to just give in and fuck him again. I think I like fucking. But he's a little too much. Emotionally. Physically, he's just right. I don't have the experience, but I do have the instinct. And it tells me that:

a) I like sex,

b) sex will only get better as I get older and more experienced, and not necessarily in that order, and

c) sex with Jovan, albeit only the tip of the iceberg, was good sex.

I'm standing at my attic room window, smoking a fag, when I see a white Saab pull into the driveway. I put on the first thing I find, my dad's old vest I sometimes sleep in, and run down the stairs.

Mum's painting the banisters at the bottom. 'For Christ's sake, put on some knickers!'

She's been so sensitive of late, I can't even smoke in my room any more without her having a go. I'm thinking her and Dad are probably getting a divorce. I'm moving in with Dad, and that's that.

Once out on the veranda, I smooth my hair over my eyes, pull down the vest, and wait. Soon enough, the gate opens to let Jovan in. He looks miserable.

'Good morning, Helena,' he says. 'I wandered here lonely as a cloud.'

'Well you shouldn't have.'

He jumps over the wooden veranda fence, grabs me by the waist and reels me in. 'You don't mean that.' He quickly discovers the true state of my undress. 'Meow-meow, pussy... Cat.'

'Get off!' I push him away. 'Why are you stalking me?'

'Because I love you.'

'Seriously, Jovan, you have got to stop.'

'You can't just stop loving a person on that person's say so.'

'What?' I remember I'm dealing with a disgraced barrister here. More slippery than a Danube eel. 'Talk straight.'

'I. Love. You.' He goes again. 'Can't get any straighter than that.'

'You're upsetting me,' I say. 'You've got to stop, you've got to stop stalking me.'

'I'm off in two days.' He looks at me funny. Like he's about to be struck by a tragedy all of his own. Sad, yeah, but not my sad. 'Fuck girl, what are you waiting for? Come with me, see the world, get to know yourself, get to know me better! What's there to consider? Nothing's set in stone, either – if you don't like, you go back home to mummy and daddy. I'm never going to stop you. I promise. What have you got to lose?'

I don't answer. It would be logical to go. Hate the school anyway. Hate this town. This country, I never felt like I belonged. Don't even start me on the people. Guys like Jovan are hard to find. Berlin's a great place. Think of the future. Blah blah.

I still ain't going. And that's another that.

He leans over. 'Helena... Honey... there's some bad shit coming. Yugoslavia is kaput. No more. Finito. You know it, I know it, everyone knows it. But not everyone will get out of its way in time. Because of the denial, mostly. Every time something bad happens, they'll say, 'Well thank God that's over and done with!' Then the next day something even worse will happen, they'll go 'Thank God! We've now seen the worst of it!' Until the shit catches up with them and it's too late to say or do anything. You know why?'

I don't answer.

'Because they'll all be dead.' He lifts his Hawaiian shirt and pulls a gun out of the back of his shorts. 'All of them.'

I wonder if he's going to shoot me. What would dying feel like. A great relief. I bet that's what the dying feel, a sense of great relief. Unless their very last living moment brings on the realisation that they will never again pick a strawberry from the garden patch, and bite into it, all red and warm from the sunshine, and have its sweet juices dribble down their chin. Oh

crap. Now I'm never going to die in peace. 'Is that for me?'

'Yep.' Jovan hands me the gun. 'Do you know how to use it?'

'Yes.' I take the gun. The Heckler & Koch P9S. I happen to know a little about guns. This one's a classic. 'My dad used to take me shooting since I was four.' I offer it back to Jovan. He shakes his head.

'You keep it.'

'I don't need a gun.'

'Fuck's sakes, Helena!' He grabs me with some force, then lets go of me as if I burnt him. 'Keep it, okay, for just in case. Please. For me. It may make a difference between–'

He chokes up. Another problem with us South Slavs : too bloody emotional. Poles and Russians, they laugh at funerals. Us, we see a single leaf falling off a tree, and we're in bits. Music starts, we cry. Music stops, we cry also. We even cry at the funeral of those we have killed. Bitter tears of South Von Slav.

'Okay,' I say. 'Thanks.'

He walks away. Just like that. He never looks back. Not once. I don't think he was really in love with me. In which case I definitely should've fucked him again.

Relationships are complicated. I feel like I'm suffocating, just talking about it. The very word, relation-ship. A ship that keeps on relating. Supposed to make sense, right. Didn't think so.

I see a crow land on the top of the chimney. I lift the gun, point it at the bird. 'Bang bang,' I say. 'You're dead.'

I always thought I was going to lose my virginity à la Esther. The Bell Jar Esther. I was looking for the right candidate, but all the ones I picked I also kind of fancied, so they didn't count. I wanted it done properly. Wham bam thank you ma'am. The minute you get your teeth into the emotional toffee-apple, you're well and truly stuck. And you stay sticky long after you left a few teeth behind in the apple, and ran for your life.

How do I even know this. I just do. It's not experience, but it never is. People pretend it's the experience that makes all the difference, but that's just another one of those socially accepted, weedy little white lies designed to justify some remote and basically unjustifiable aspect of human existence. I'm not sure how I know this, either. But I do. I just do. Besides, if human experience ever made any real difference, then what's up with all the wars no one ever wins, no one could ever win.

And what's up with all the talk of the war coming to Vukovar. I can't imagine this ever manifesting outside the whispering corridors of the disempowered populace. Then again, what if I'm right, like I usually am, and the lack of human ability to learn, from their own experience as well as that of another, does indeed manifest into the heart of my degenerate little world as some terrible monster, intended on inflicting endless torment until there's nothing else left to live for. Or could it be that the Powers That Be designed a plan to sacrifice this corner of the world so that the greater good can be accomplished. Yeah, that must be it. I'd bet my bottom dollar on it, except I'm fresh out.

Fuck. Five days in the house prison, and I'm already thinking like a prisoner. As if anyone gives a shit about Vukovar, or even knows where we are on the great map of the Universe. Let alone plots to sacrifice it; we're hardly sacrificial lamb material, we're not that innocent.

MOTHER'S LITTLE SECRET

Jovan left today. He never did phone again. Nor visited. Well, I guess he had served his purpose. I am very glad I remembered to ask for the second fuck that morning. I'm glad I didn't just run away, like I always do.

Wonder if losing your virginity in a blackout counts as the existentialist leap of non-faith par excellence. I hope so. I really do. Because, I don't like fucking up on a good plan, and as this is not something you can easily revisit, I have no other choice but reach the verdict that I did far better than the poor mad pathetic Esther could've ever achieved in that precious, poetry addled, tender life of hers.

Day Nine. Or it could be Twelve. Lost count. All I know is that Jovan has left, Lazar stayed away and Iva hasn't called for ages. The last time she phoned, and I sort of answered by lifting the receiver and saying nothing, she let out a mighty, earth-shattering sigh, then hung up on me. How rude.

A few other people still call. I ignore them, mostly because I think they are idiots. I only pretended I liked them so I didn't look lonely, so I got invited to their parties. Can't believe I was ever that shallow. On the other hand, sometimes only the shallow will do, and I may well do it again.

But not today I don't think. I am beyond depressed. Think the word is bored. It doesn't help any that I start my day by waking up far too early. Four o'clock in the morning. Or half past five. It's as if I wake up on some invisible, inaudible cue. As if something brings me out of my sweet slumber, and suddenly I'm sitting up in bed, alert and waiting for something else to happen. Wondering if this is Death itself, announcing its final call. Final for me, that is. Then I read one of my dad's numerous books on alternative medicine, the one on traditional Chinese medicine, and discovered something called the 24hr Body Qi Cycle. It's very interesting, even if it probably is a load of bollocks. Still, according to this so called Cycle, each organ meridian has a two-hour period when qi is at its peak. Qi is like their word for energy that's supposed to keep us alive. Life-force, I think they call it – you're fine if you have it, dead if you don't. Anyway, 3–5am is lung time, 5–7am large intestine. Both of these organs seem to connect with the emotion of grief, of letting go. Which is a bit of a let-down as far as acceptable theories go, because, whatever else may be going on, nobody's died. Except for my godfather. But nobody else. So what's there for me to grieve for.

I wait for my parents to bugger off to work, then go downstairs for breakfast.

I have a pot of Turkish coffee, chased by at least three

cigarettes, before the yawning kicks in. I grab a sheet, a book, my smoking paraphernalia consisting of a large crystal ashtray, half-full box of *Bijela Drina* and a lighter, and head off for the deckchair. 'Shoo you beast!' I shake Miko off the chair, but he's laying low, holding on for dear life. 'Shoo! I'm asking you nicely, so shoo!' He gives me pair of emerald green daggers, before jumping off, his tail a-flailing. He's so going to come back to seek his revenge, I know he is. That's one of the reasons I carry the sheet, so I can cover myself head to toe. If nothing pokes out, then he doesn't have anything to provoke him out of his tiny little mind. Another reason is that I cannot just lie there without something on me. No matter how hot or humid. I have to have a cover. 'Safety blanket,' as Teodora calls it. Wittily. Talking of which, the witch has gone off to the Adriatic Coast with a gaggle of her slutty friends. It's good not to have her around and I wish she never comes back.

I settle down with my book, nothing too genius. Kerouac. On The Road. Lots of men, pretending they're clever and important. Not that I'm a feminist, or anything. But men are good at taking themselves seriously. So the women like them better. And women, why would they fall for this macho crap I'll never understand. I open the book and fall fast asleep.

I look out of my half-shut eyelids. Everything's white. Birds are singing some place high above. I smile, then pull the sheet off. Miko's on me before I can even wipe that smile off my face. He bites into the fleshy bit underneath my left thumb. Not too hard, just hard enough for me to go, 'You fuck!'

Somebody laughs. I turn around and see Mum. She's wearing a bikini.

I have never seen Mum in a bikini before. She is not that fat.

'What time is it?' I ask.

She checks her wristwatch. 'Almost eleven.'

'Why are you here?'

'Why is anyone?'

'I mean, why are you not at work?'

'Because I'd rather lie here on our lovely outside sofa and sunbathe, than sit in the office reading my novel under the desk, pretending to work.'

We have an outside sofa, yes. And an outside armchair, too. They live in our summer kitchen but people keep dragging them out. Very nice, except that I once had a dream in which I was lying on that very sofa, almost exactly in the same position my mum's in now, and I was just watching the clouds go by and generally minding my own business. Suddenly, I could feel this warm damp patch spreading underneath me, so I jumped off and saw the sofa was covered in blood. I looked into my knickers, and nope, it wasn't me. And if it wasn't me, then it must've been the sofa, the sofa was bleeding! I freaked out, yet at the same time I felt compelled to investigate further. I sneaked up to the sofa, touched the now softly bubbling fountain of blood. My fingers went deeper, and deeper, and I could feel my hand touching inside of the sofa, examining its guts. I wanted to pull it out and run away, but I just couldn't. My arm was elbow deep in the sofa blood and guts before I finally managed to yank myself out and scramble away, back into the corner of my bedroom, naked and bloody and crying hard.

I have never sat on that sofa ever again since. I avoid the armchair, too. In fact, I avoid all upholstered furniture. I'd rather sit on people's beds, or if that won't do, their kitchen chairs. I say my back prefers it that way. Like some old person.

Talking of old, I wonder what's up with Mum. She's never home from work early. Frankly, I don't like this. It's weird. Sunbathing with your own mother.

In the garden. On a weekday. Maybe she's sick.

'Are you sick?'

'I was,' she says. 'But I'm not any more.'

I need a pee. 'Would you like me to bring you something from the house? A camomile tea?'

'There is a plate of coconut fingers in the larder, fancy sharing? And a beer?'

A beer? 'Really?'

'Oh yes,' she says. 'Please.'

I go in, kind of dazed. I never did understand that woman. And I think she's getting harder to read the older she gets. Not easier. Her moods for example. One moment she's all lovey-dovey with the world, the next she's flipped right out of her socket, and over the most minute detail ever. Like the other day, when Dad returned from the market with a couple of shiny golden carp. Naturally, he placed them in the downstairs tub. But Mum went mad. So mad, in fact, she burst into tears and wouldn't speak to anyone for the rest of that day. No one asked why. No one dared. Where are we supposed to leave carp from now on, if

133

the bathtub is suddenly out of bounds? No one knows.

That bloody woman. She's now ruined my quiet day in. One of my many quiet days in – this must be some kind of a record. Truth be told, I miss going out. Yet at the same time, the very idea of going out there, drinking, talking, hanging, well it makes me feel suicidal. I'd like to go back to how I was only a few months ago. Never home, except to sleep and get a change of clothes. Always running away. To Iva's. To town. To parties. To drink. To find a man to have sex with for the first time. So exciting, it was. My life was like a kaleidoscope, and now it's no more. Now it is nothing. And even that is about to be destroyed. I know it is. It's not what people say, they always predict the worst. It's about how I feel. About these sticky black wisps floating around in the air, like threads of a broken web belonging to a giant pissed off spider. He's coming to get us. He knows where we are. He's coming for his revenge. There's no way out. So no point in running and hiding.

Well at least I can have a beer. She said I could. She'd better not take it back.

'Here you go, Mother.' I place the tray on the round wooden table in front. I call Mum mother on very rare occasions. It's a joke. Although I don't think anyone actually laughs out loud. Not that kind of a joke. I glance at her, check for any sign of a possible mind change upon seeing the two bottles of beer on the tray. Not sure what she said back there. Share the fingers, but she'd also like a beer vs share the fingers, and share a beer vs share the fingers, and a beer each.

Hmm. Too many question marks to even count.

Obviously, I chose the very latter. If something does go wrong, I can always have a beer in secret. Yeah. If I really wanted to. 'Cheers,' I say, and bite into a finger. It's soft and sweet, very coconutty. Not to mention it goes surprisingly well with beer. 'Yum.'

Mum brings the bottle to her lips, then lowers it back onto the table. Untouched. She then stares at the mid-distance for a while. Which I find pretty unnerving. I light up, looking braver than I feel. You never know what the moody person will do next. Or tell you to do next. One minute I can smoke as much as I'm bloody well entitled to, anywhere I bloody well like, the next I'm being told I smoke too much, and therefore can only smoke outside from then onwards. Well, we're outside now. Very unsettling, having a moody for a mother. I may well be scarred for life.

I take another deep drag on my cigarette, soothe myself a little. Mum slaps her hand over her mouth, leaps off the outside sofa and runs over to the rose bushes. She just about makes it before she starts throwing up all over them. I shall never smell a flower again for as long as I live.

She drags herself back to the sofa. I go in and bring back a glass of water, and a few paper napkins. She takes them in a grateful way, I would say. I hazard a quick glance. Her face is sort of patchy red, yet also sort of naked. In an almost pretty way. She's crying.

'There,' I offer her the water. 'It's okay.'

'Thank you, Helena.' She gives me a rueful smile. 'My darling abstract daughter.'

No need for personal comments, I don't think,

especially after somebody's gone out of their way to help you. 'Do you mean me?'

She rolls her eyes. 'Yes, I mean you. Teodora is my little terracotta warrior. You, on the other hand, you're made with hardly any earth, you're all water and fire and air.'

I quickly compare and contrast, decide that all things considered, I'd rather not be likened to a terracotta pot. Haaaha. Teodora will not be liking this.

'It is you I worry about,' she says. 'That's why I've been so angry with you lately.'

'So I noticed.'

She laughs. 'Sorry.'

'But why? What have I done?'

'It's not anything you did do, not this time. It what you didn't do – you didn't go away with Jovan. It's that simple.'

I stand there, dumbfounded not only by this strange and deeply uncomfortable heart to heart we seem to be having, but also the information database she has on my life. Spies, every single one of them. 'How did you know?'

'Mothers,' she says. 'We know everything.'

Yeah right. 'Why would you want me to leave with him? You don't even know him.'

'He's a nice man. I could tell he is. And he has feelings for you. Plans. You had a man with a plan, and you let him go – how could you do such a thing?'

'Easy. I'm not in love with him.'

She throws her head right back, lets out a raspy laugh. 'Love? It has nothing to do with it.'

'You must be shit-kidding me.' Her, of all people, sneering at love. 'The romantic fiction Queen of Slavonija & Srijem.'

'That's exactly where romance belongs,' she says. 'Real life's an entirely different story.'

My heart hardens. 'Just because you never loved Daddy!'

Mum shrugs. She shrugs. 'That's not what I said. You should've gone off with Jovan when you had a chance. Now what am I supposed to do with you?'

'What do you mean, do with me?' I'm starting to sound pretty dumb, and I blame her for it. 'I don't follow.'

She swings out her hand and lands a hard slap on the back of my thigh. 'Ouch!' What's with all this proclivity towards physical abuse and violence against my person.

'Wake up, Helena! We'll all have to leave this place sooner or later! And I don't know where we willll go, when the time comes, I'm not sure what we're going to do.'

'I'm not going anywhere!'

'Yes, you are!'

'No! And you can't make me!'

'Oh really? So you'll stay here, wait for the soldiers to march in? Chetniks, mercenaries, paramilitary… So that they can all take turns in raping you, then shoot you in the head when they've had enough?'

'You're horrible!' I jump to my feet and make to leave, but she grabs my wrist. 'Let go!' But the woman seems to possess a grip of steel. 'I hate you!'

'Helena, I'm sorry! I'm so sorry, honey…' She lets

go so suddenly, I'm sent flying into the old quince tree. I open my mouth, about to tell her the most hurtful thing I could think of, but the woman is crying so hard I don't think she'd even hear me. 'So sorry...'

I pick myself off the ground, dust off, straighten up. It just doesn't make sense for anyone to get this worried on the strength of some second-rate warmongering. I really don't know what's going on here, but I know one thing: somebody must be dying. 'Mum? What's the matter? Please tell me.'

It takes her a few long minutes to gather her wits, blow her nose, cry a little more, smooth down her hair. Smoothing down of the hair is a very important part of getting on with it. You never see a cat walking around with its hairs all ruffled up. Bet that would be just too disorientating. If Miko is being naughty, I sometimes pull his tail, then pretend it wasn't me. And if he's being especially bad, I run my hand up his fur, and leave it like that, so he has to interrupt his own train of thought, sit down and lick himself smooth. He hates this even more than the raindrops.

Eventually, she looks up, pats the place on the sofa next to her. Is this day never going to end. But I go sit, don't want to make her cry again. 'Is somebody dying?'

She smiles and messes up my hair, like I was a boy. 'No Helena, nobody's dying.' Then what. 'I'm pregnant. You're going to have a little brother or sister.'

'Does Dad know?'

That's all I could think of saying. She laughs. I laugh. Oh how we laugh.

BUKOWSKI'S MIDGET

Knock me down with a feather. After such a major announcement, all I could do is leave. Politely. And therefore not before offering to:

a) make a jar of lemonade,

b) help her go inside,

c) bring out her books,

d) fry her a couple of eggs, and

e) go down the garden and pick some fresh mint in case the nausea returns to sender.

She circled none of the above, so I handed over my sincere congratulations and left. I didn't mean it, of course. The congratulations. A baby brother or sister – at my age. Oh God. That's just horrible. Truly selfish thing to do to me. Cruel. Bit revolting, too. Can't bear thinking of. I find my way to the bottom step on the Danube promenade, check around for any river snakes, sunbathing on warm concrete blocks, then sit down and stare at the other side. The Serbian side. There's only this river in between. Fancy that. God I'm tired. Emotionally exhausted. But also physically knackered. Walked all the way to Iva's, but she was out. That's all her mum would divulge. What's with the bloody mothers and their secret-service attitude all of a sudden.

'She's out on important family business,' she said.

Iva, family business, in the same sentence. Well now I've heard it all. I noticed her mum was watching me like a hawk. As if she was waiting for me to say the wrong thing, make the wrong move. There was a little red and white chequered badge, a symbol of Croatian independence from the rest of Yugoslavia, just above her heart. She tapped it with her finger, as if to inform my darkly byzantine Serbian ancestors that there's more where she came from. Are these people even for real. And what's happened to Iva. Have her parents sold her soul to the devil. Or has she done it herself. I've never felt so totally, irrevocably separated from somebody I used to like. And hate. But mostly like, and get on with. All because we're all of a sudden supposed to be different from one another. Says who.

I couldn't get away from Iva's house quickly enough. I was so angry. I know what the real different feels like, looks like, how it can shun you, push you, shove you, make you cry yourself to sleep naked in the corner of your bedroom. And stuff. This difference, this so-called Serbo-Croat-Muslim difference, it's not for real and I will never ever believe their stupid lies, and I will never understand why anyone would, not if I lived for a thousand years.

I know what it's like to be different from everyone else, okay. Pretending you're just like them, waiting around and even praying for a friend. A real friend, someone you don't have to play it down, or play it up with all the fucking time. You could just stick to playing for a change. Have fun, kill time, stick around, get drunk, have a laugh with. Even if they annoy you, especially if they annoy you. I hate most people, that much is true, but still I don't see much point in living life devoid of love. And hate. But mostly love.

'I wish I brought my swimming trunks.'

I look up, see this man I sort of know from around town, standing next to me, sheltering his eyes from the sun as he's inspecting the other side. Everyone loves the other side. Must be its grass.

'You can always skinny-dip.'

'You reckon?' He sits next to me. Who said he could do that. 'How long before I'm charged with an indecent exposure?'

I don't answer. This man's unnerving me. He's sitting too close to me, for starters. It's different now that I'm no longer a virgin. I'm different. That bloody word again. Talking of different, this man is not very tall. And when I say not very tall, I mean he's practically a midget. He sure knows what different feels like. I pretend I'm looking south, but actually throw a reasonably long glance across his face. Handsome. Pale skin, jet black hair, those dark eyes kind of sleepily burning a hole in you. Doesn't sound good, this burning/dark combination, but it does look good. Poetic and passionate. I reckon I could fall in love with him, maybe, providing he grew up a bit. Literally.

'What's your name?'

'Helena.'

He offers his hand. I accept. It's a nice hand. Normal size. Firm. I get a flashback of Jovan, pressing himself against me, making his way in between my thighs. I blush. Christ. Am I a nymphomaniac now. 'I'm Buk.'

'Vuk?'

'No, Buk. Short for Bukowski. My favourite author. Guess I quoted him once too often, ended up with the nickname.'

'I love Bukowski.'

'No way!'

I look at him straight this time. 'Yes way.'

'Sorry,' he goes. 'It's just, I've never met a girl who was into Bukowski... What book did you read?'

'Umm, Post Office, Factotum... Ham on Rye of course, Women...'

'Wow!' He takes my hand. Not exactly snatches it, but nevertheless reaches out and takes it without asking. Then he kisses it. Christ. 'I am beyond impressed.'

I wriggle my hand out of his over the top grip. 'Because I can read?'

'Not only beautiful and clever, but funny, too!' He laughs, no doubt to illustrate his er witty point. 'Have I just met the perfect girl?'

'There's no such thing.' I say, even though I don't mean it. I am the perfect girl, but I don't trust he can actually grasp this.

He changes tack. 'Sorry, didn't mean to patronise. It's just, I really have never met a girl who'd read Charlie, let alone liked him.'

Charlie, is it. How very... Midgety. He's right, though. Even Iva says Bukowski's a dirty old man. Which is true, to a point, but he's also a poet. A great poet at that. Plus he likes his drink. I like that. I like it

142

that he runs to his scotch and his poetry and his skunky women no matter whether the going gets tough or easy. His birthday's one day after my dad's. Wish my dad was more like Bukowski. Anyway… My point is, I wouldn't necessarily drink with Charles Bukowski, but I would drink in his name. 'Have you read Hollywood?'

I shake my head. 'It's not out in the library yet.'

'I have it,' says Buk. 'The best translation ever, Belgrade of course, fresh off the press.'

'And the book? Any good?'

He thinks about it. 'Mmmm, well… why don't I lend it to you and then maybe we could compare notes afterwards?'

'Really?' I would never lend a book to a stranger. Or to anyone really, not since Teodora gave my precious copy of Jules and Jim as a present to this random boy who was visiting from Vienna, no doubt frog-marched by his parents to start making friends with his ten-times-removed redneck cousins. He was one of those old-fashioned gastarbeiter kids, mum and dad working and saving hard for decades some place Germanic so they can return to their village in style. One day, maybe next year, or the one after that. Meanwhile, the kids, well they just grow up thinking they're German, or Austrian, or whatever. Until they get a very rude awakening when, usually half-way down the autobahn on what they think is just another unbearable but fleeting annual visit to their so-called roots, their parents go, 'Surprise, little Klaus, we've burnt our

143

Ausweis and there's no going back to that capitalist filth ever again!' They've been around for as long as I remember, these limbo kids, struggling to get by on their funky pigeon Serbo-Croat, having to adjust to the climate of the land that time forgot, and standing in for a German teacher when he couldn't be bothered to do his job.

So Teodora sees this boy, he's reading a book in a foreign language, and she runs all the way home, steals the book from my own private bookshelf, then goes off to impress. Make him believe she's anything other than what she really is – a sheep, and a white one at that. Come to think of it, that's how I discovered that I hated her. The revelation came with a sense of relief. There was no more need to feel guilty, or to pretend I felt otherwise. A fair deal, especially because the book can and will be replaced. Peace of mind, not so easily.

'Absolutely,' says Buk. 'What are you up to right now?'

'Nothing much.'

'Tell you what,' he says. 'How about we go to mine to get the book, and maybe chill a little, hmm...? Smoke some dope, listen to Jimi Hendrix, what do you say?'

I don't know about no Jimi Hendrix, but:

a) I have nothing better to do,

b) it's been ages since I smoked dope, or did anything remotely illegal, and

c) spoke with someone half-intelligent who wasn't Iva. Or Jovan. Or Lazar.

'Count me in,' I say.

He gets up, helps me to my feet. We stand next to each other for a moment. Fuck this guy is short.

Buk's place is not really his place. Surprise surprise. Everyone lives with their parents around here. People in Yugoslavia are not exactly encouraged to grow up. Like my own father, for example, who actually chose to build the house on his own father's land, just around the corner from where he grew up. Charles Bukowski would never do any such thing. See. Different mentality altogether, despite their birthdays being so close.

So Buk's place is basically a large room built across the yard from his parents' house. Except it turns out his mum died at birth. Apparently he was a really big baby.

'Ironic, right,' he says.

I am not sure what to say here. 'So... Your father brought you up, then?'

'Not sure I'd put it like that.' He unlocks his room, lets me in. It's very dark in here. I can smell books. 'He's a drunkard. Blamed me for Mum's death. Still does. So I was brought up by my grandmother – and these good people.' He puts on the light, points at his book collection. And what a collection it is. There are bookshelves floor to ceiling, wall to wall. Filled with books, not ornaments and crap. There's also a bed. That's about it, except for a record player in the corner, with a row of records neatly stacked up next to it. And a small portable TV on top of a tiny coffee table. Oh – and a knackered green armchair in the middle of the room. 'My girlfriend was here last night. She wanted to fuck right there in that chair.' He grins. 'She's sex mad. I like that in a girl.'

I pretend to be engrossed in the book titles. Now he's talking sex, why didn't he talk sex when we were still out in the open. Is this what men do, play silly games. Do not like games. I'd rather people would just come out and say, 'Hello how's your pussy doing today? Want some company down there?' Then you have an option of saying yes or no. Or even maybe. Without feeling like somebody's trying to trick you.

'Yes,' Buk says. 'These are my real parents. Every single one, I owe them part of my life. Would you like something to drink?'

'Yes, please!'

'Great! I'm just going to pop over to see my old man. He's probably fast asleep by now, he'll be no trouble. Wine okay?'

I nod.

'Back in a minute. Make yourself at home.'

'I will, thanks.'

No I won't. I'm just going to have a glass of wine, get that book and get the fuck out. Maybe I won't even get the book, so I don't have to return here ever again. I don't even want the joint any more. What am I doing, holing up with strange men like this. Maybe I'm some kind of a slut, just like my sister.

I decide to take a look at Buk's ahem parents. He's taking himself way too seriously, especially for a midget. William Faulkner. Ernest Hemingway. Marguerite Duras. Dylan Thomas. F. Scott Fitzgerald. Jack Kerouac. All the pissheads. Virginia Woolf. Hermann Hesse. Sylvia Plath. Norman Mailer. The depressives. Salman Rushdie. Fyodor Dostoyevsky. The assholes. Quite predictable, really.

'So what do you think?' Buk's back, carrying a couple of bottles of wine and a plate of half-moon biscuits covered in vanilla sugar. 'Hungry?'

I am, as it happens. 'Not really.' I don't know why I keep doing this. Think one thing, say another. But I do. And anyway, it is not as if Buk and I are best mates, like I need to tell him everything I think, or feel. There's nothing wrong with keeping myself a mystery. 'I'll have that glass of wine, though.'

'Of course you will.' He deposits his loot in the middle of the floor, points at the Fucking Chair. 'Please, sit.'

I don't think so. I sit on the bed.

'Even better,' he says. This man obviously thinks everything's about him. Maybe it's because he's so little. He smiles. There's something of a young Robert De Niro about this guy, of the Taxi Driver intensity. He passes me a glass of red wine. I take a sip. Yuk. Never liked the taste of alcohol. As if reading my mind, or maybe just my face, Buk says, 'Not exactly your finest vintage, but it's all my old man had stashed away, besides a bottle of *rakija*. Didn't think you'd be interested in that.'

Rakija is a very strong spirit, made either out of plums or grapes. It tastes disgusting and I hate it. It was drinking *rakija* from a little tin cup attached to the wooden barrel in Iva's cellar that had made me pee myself in the middle of our kitchen, for all to see. I don't even remember how I got home, or why I didn't stay at Iva's, like I did every other time I got smashed.

All I remember is coming round in the middle of the kitchen, with a puddle already spreading around my feet. Dad saying, 'Oh my, think I'd better leave this with you,' then walking out, leaving me alone with Mum. She was saying something, too, but I buggered off into my bedroom, stripped off, and just about managed to hit my beloved corner before I passed out. Not a happy memory. And if I'm completely honest, still slightly mortifying.

'Is your dad really an alcoholic?'

Buk laughs. 'Why? Do you think I'd invent something like that?'

I shrug. 'I don't know about you, but I would.'

He stops doing what he was doing, which was making the biggest fattest joint

I have ever seen, gives me a good long look. 'You are for real, I know you are, but can I still touch you, just to make sure?'

I play it cool. 'Sure you can.'

He squats in front of me, takes in my face, then kind of smooths down my eyebrows, my jawline, and my collarbone. Sends a crazy shiver down my spine. 'You're real alright. Who would've thought.' Buk goes back to his joint making factory in the middle of the floor. I take another sip of my wine. Yuk. I need a cigarette to disguise the taste. Perhaps I will take a biscuit after all. I do, and it tastes melt-in-the-mouth scrumptious. I want to eat more, finish them off in fact, except that would never do.

'Do you know any of these writers?' Buk asks. 'Not many women, are there?' He sniggers.

I know why he sniggered. Women only ever write

about love. And about men. And worst of all, children. Marguerite Duras could just about get away with it, on account of being a magnificent writer, and not at all snivelly when it came to love and sex and relationships. When I was really little, I used to read Francoise Sagan. I blame it on a sudden infiltration by my mum's genes. Didn't last long, my Sagan stage. She was just too annoying.

Buk lights up the joint. He looks like a rabbit who's just caught himself a big fat carrot. I finish off my wine. 'Tell me, Helena, who is your favourite writer?'

'Selma Lagerlöf.'

'Selma Lagerlöf?'

I lean over and take the joint out of his hand. 'Yeah. Do you know her?'

He smiles as wide as a Cheshire cat. 'Do I know her. Gösta Berling is probably my favourite literary character ever!'

Exclamation mark. I hate it when people speak like this. Exclamation mark, question mark, inverted commas. Words are meant to run free, not get weighed down by fancy equipment. I take a toke, and instantly realise this is a very different story from the joints Iva and I used to make with the weed we stole from her brother. 'Really?' I hear myself say. 'I want to marry him.'

Buk shuffles over and lays his head on my leg. 'You don't marry someone you can live with, you marry the person you can't live without – you know who said this?'

'Not a clue.'

'Me neither.' Buk nibbles on my thigh. I'm not

averse to this, per se, what I am averse to is having a relationship with a midget. Plus, I don't need no additional complications in my life right now. Men. One fuck, and they want to marry you. Underneath all that bravado, they just want to hold your hand, or rather they want to have their hand held onto. Men are relationship freaks. One fuck, and you're going steady. A few fucks later still and you're walking down the aisle, unless of course you've been watching your step like a hawk all along and avoided all the pitfalls. Exhausting business, men.

'Hey,' I say. 'What about your girlfriend?'

'What about her?'

'That chair over there is still smoking hot, remember?'

'I don't care about Maja. Not any more.' He pushes his head in between my legs, takes a deep breath. 'Now this is what I call nectar.'

Would it be so bad if I slept with Buk. Would it make any difference if I didn't. Most importantly, do I have anyone better to sleep with. Then it dawns on me. 'Are you re-enacting one of Bukowski's stories?'

He thinks for a bit. 'Shit. I don't know. Maybe I am.'

'Well don't.'

He moves away. 'You're right. You deserve an authentic treatment, none of this second-hand shit.'

'And more wine.'

'Of course.' Buk turns to pour the wine, I grab another biscuit. Nectar indeed. 'Have another toke, this is a good stuff, Moroccan, straight off the ship.'

I'm guessing he means the ships that stop in

Vukovar for a little sleepover on their way up or down Danube. And a spot of trading in illegal substances. I see those sailors around town. They all look like prison inmates. Every single one of them. I pretend not to see them, just like my mum taught me. She also taught me to never turn around if anyone wolf-whistles after me. I don't know what that's all about. It's only natural to turn around, check who's making so much noise. I see that I need to break some more rules. A girl's work is never done.

WE USED TO BE FRIENDS

I fall onto the floor. Tiles are cold and hard, my head is the last part of my body to hit them. It doesn't hurt. The clouds must've cushioned the impact. White fluffy clouds, this is where I'll live from now on. Cloud nine thousand and ninety-nine. My new address, take note, everyone. And just as I'm starting to enjoy myself, the front page of tomorrrow's Vukovar Weekly flashes right in front of my closed eyes: *Daughter of a prominent University professor found dead from a suspected weed overdose in a dingy downtown bathroom.*

Fuck, goes my very last remaining thinking molecule.

I know I'm some place strange, again, no need to open my eyes. In situations like these, I've found it best to slowly feel my way around my immediate surroundings. I came round like this on the top of a scaffolding once, so I know what I'm talking about. It's soft here, and it's warm, I'm guessing it's a bed. Phew. Helena lives another day.

Next, I do a quick body scan. Pain – check. No pain's always a promising sign. Clothes on – check. Although not a slut, unlike some (Teodora), I have this habit of stripping off when drunk or distressed, but not necessarily when taking a shower. I've been pretty lucky no one's raped me thus far, as Iva likes to remind me. Not that I can remember, is what I think but never say. Shoes – check. Shoes being off are usually a sure sign that:

a) somebody else is there with you, and

b) they probably mean you no harm.

So I open my eyes, a tiny little bit. Because I'm feeling paranoid, but also in case somebody's watching me. There are candles everywhere, bouncing the shadows around a group of people sitting in a circle in the middle of the room. A sect's got me. I will now most probably have to sleep with the devil himself, and bear his baby. Ew. How I hate babies. On the other hand, I wouldn't have to look after it – the sect would do that. And I could ask for whatever I want on account of being the devil baby's mother. Me, a mother, to a baby. Can't bear thinking about. So why am I. Then it dawns on me. My bloody mother. I can't believe her. Dad, too. What were they even doing, doing it. Christ. I feel sick. May need to puke, but first I must establish Where In The World. I glance left, I glance right. Books. Hmm. I think I've been here before.

One of the shapes on the floor moves, turns over a record. It's either Jimi Hendrix, or The Doors. I always get these two mixed up. Who cares. I don't. What's important is to get out of here. I want to go home. My heart misses a beat. It's the word, home. Does something to me every time.

My nose starts itching bad. I scratch it, but not stealthily enough.

'Hey, Sleeping Beauty!' Buk lifts a candlestick, points it in my general direction. 'Welcome back.'

Everyone looks up. I don't want to be here. I get up and start looking for my shoes. 'How embarrassing,' I do the usual time-filler whilst looking for an escape route. 'To fall asleep like that. I'm ever so sorry.' I see my shoes, slip them on and am ready to roll out of here. 'Thanks for your hospitality, and everything, I'd better be off home, so, er, my mum doesn't send a search party.'

'She needs to have some water,' someone says.

'And sugar,' another adds. 'You don't want her passing out on the street.'

'I never pass out,' I say. 'I'll be fine.'

Buk stands in front of me. I could step over him if I really had to. I keep my options open. 'You did pass out earlier on. In the bathroom. That joint was probably a little too strong for you.'

Somebody laughs. 'You didn't give her an untempered joint, did you, Buk? She's, like, twelve, you greedy fuck.'

'Eighteen, actually,' I lie, and for no good reason. Owning up to being sixteen could've at least put these guys off raping me for another two years. I do make my own self wonder sometimes. Like for example, what is it I really want to get out of life. But mostly how to get out of a bad situation before it gets worse.

'Yeah, well, that joint might've been a bit of a missile, sorry, Helena,' Buk says. 'Five minutes, okay… Have a biscuit, a sip of water, and I'll walk you home.'

154

Like hell you will. I'm now upset with Buk on two accounts:

a) because he let me have a real strong joint, just so he could impress me or seduce me better, and

b) because he exposed my weakness in front of his loser mates. Seriously: there are four of them, and they're all wearing bottle-bottom glasses. So may I please call them losers now.

The thing is, I do feel slightly queasy. I give the motley another look. Seems like I've interrupted a chess tournament, which would fit nicely in with the glasses. There are a couple of books left lying wide open on the floor. I bet it's poetry. I look in closer, and sure enough, it's Baudelaire – and Akhmatova. Go figure. I sit down, just outside the circle, then pour myself some fizzy water. I smell it first, in case it's *rakija*, then take a sip. Safe.

'Hello,' says one of the losers. 'I'm Petar.'

Oh who cares. I extend my hand. Being polite keeps people at bay. It's the most useful tool for anyone with antisocial tendencies. By the end of this meeting & greeting session, I have four new friends, or at least that's what they're thinking. They are called Petar, Doktor, Bobo and Kit. I take the last biscuit from the plate, ask what they do. Kit and Bobo are librarians; of course they are. I sort of remember seeing them around the library, not that I ever paid them any real attention. To me, library assistants are like robots, there to fetch the books. I kind of wish they stayed that way. Now they'll want me to make small talk and shit. Doktor is a consultant at Vukovar hospital. A gynaecologist. He looks quite embarrassed when he tells me what he does for a living, and I think rightly so. Poking around people's cunts all day long, what sort of person chooses a life full of that.

Petar is a little harder to pinpoint. It's as if he hasn't got a profession. Not a real one, at least. Which I know could be done in the West, what with all the amazing social provisions and lavish student grants and fantastic art programs, but I've never known anyone who got away with it in Yugoslavia. Everyone here assumes a clear cut role pretty early on in their life, and holds it for posterity. Like in a game of statues, but not one I'd like to take part in. And it seems like Petar wouldn't, either. Accordingly, he's keeping himself animated by performing in an up-and-coming heavy metal band as both lead vocal and lead guitar, as well as writing all their music and lyrics. In addition, he's a semi-professional cyclist. His club used to send him to race abroad all the time, less often now because he is too busy with the kids' theatre club he also happens to run. Is this man some kind of a saint, then. I know it doesn't make any sense, but I feel far more impressed with Petar, whom I have little in common, than with Buk, with whom I share this great love of all things literary. It's not that I have a crush on Petar, either. It's just... I don't know. Something about him.

'You should go West,' I tell him. 'Start living for real.'

He removes a lock of dark hair out of his face, smiles in a cool-person way. 'My life's real enough.'

'It can't get any more real, renting a room off your parents,' says Bobo. 'The little one's right, you have the talent, you have more than one talent, you lucky fuck, go offer it some place where it will be appreciated.'

'Screw the integrity,' says Kit. 'So overrated.'

'Yeah,' says Doktor. 'Go for dineros.'

'I like it here,' says Petar. 'I like you guys. I like my band. I like the river.' He glances towards me. 'Not to mention the girls.'

Must every man I meet falls in love with me. 'I would go tomorrow, if I could.'

'Where to?' asks Petar.

'Ideally? Paris. Or London. Not really bothered, as long as it's West.'

'West is best,' says Kit. 'You go, girl.'

'Exactly,' I say. 'They don't judge you just because of the clothes you wear, and you get a proper chance to go places if you have a talent. Here, it's all about who you know.'

'Have you been abroad before?' asks Bobo.

Suddenly, I feel out of my depth. They're all like, old, and more experienced than me. Yet just look at them all, a sect of wasted life and missed opportunity. All except Petar, that is. He still has some life left in him. 'Yes, Paris and Trieste, and Venice, and Bratislava. Oh, and I've been to Budapest.'

'The last two don't really count,' says Doktor. 'Both cities being in Eastern Europe.'

Clever counting, Doctor Cunt.

'He said abroad,' I say.

'If you want to go West,' says Buk. 'Now's your time.'

I hate it when somebody says something, and everyone goes quiet like this, like what they said is the truth, the whole truth and nothing but the truth, and cannot be changed nor challenged. 'Why?'

As expected, they all turn to me, incredulous.

'Why now?' I repeat.

'Are you kidding?' says Buk. He's suddenly sounding less poetic, more, what's the word. Peasanty. 'The air's so thick with the talk of war, you can cut it with a knife and feed it to your pigs.'

'It's only gossip,' I say.

'Come on, child!' Buk lights up a cigarette, which for some reason instantly makes him look a little more intelligent and a lot taller. No wonder so many men choose to smoke. 'Slovenia and Croatia want to separate from Yugoslavia, which is not something the Serbs will ever allow to happen, not without a fight.'

'It's only politicians,' I say. 'Warmongering. So don't vote for them.'

'Too right I'll vote for them,' says Buk. 'I'll vote for anyone who promises to keep those two stuck up republics from just taking off and leaving, not after all that Tito did to keep this country together.'

'But he's dead.' I'm not sure why I even go there. Buk's getting on my nerves, so that's probably why. What's with the aggression, when only a few hours ago he swore that all he ever wanted to do is write. And fuck. In peace.

'What do you mean?' Buk seems cagey. 'So what if he's dead?'

'Well, Yugoslavia didn't exactly belong to him.'

They all stare at me again, as if I've said something amazing. Someone sniggers. Kit, I think.

'Out of the mouth of babes...' says Bobo.

'Bollocks!' says Doktor. 'She has no idea what she's talking about.'

'Actually,' says Petar. 'Tito did create Yugoslavia, then held it together by the sheer power of his personal myth, right? Is it any wonder it's all falling apart now that he's dead? I think what we're talking about here is evolution in action.'

'Fuck evolution,' says Doktor. 'Give me a revolution any time.'

Even to my untrained little political eye, it is clear that Doktor and Buk are Serbs, Petar also. Bobo could be a Croat. Or a Serb. Possibly a Muslim. Kit I have no clue about. Oh bollocks. That's the problem with the South Slavs, they all look the same, even as they aim their guns at one another. Or maybe especially then.

I yawn.

'Enough politics,' says Buk. 'We're boring the lady.'

I see my exit opportunity, and grab it by the throat. 'Oh gosh, I really must be going...' I stand up and offer everyone a girly wave. 'Nice to have met you all.' I step over the chess board. 'May the best man win, and all that...'

Buk catches up with me at the door. 'You don't need to go,' he whispers. 'I can get rid of them... Stay.'

Like fuck I will. 'Thanks for the offer, but no. Got to get home, see.'

Petar joins us. 'Thanks, Buk, great evening.' He turns to me. 'Would you like a lift?'

'Yes please!'

Buk looks green with a combination of envy, jealousy and bad lighting. 'I was about to walk Helena home.'

Petar gives me a quizzical look. 'I'll go with Petar,' I confirm. 'But again, thanks for the offer.'

Once outside on the dark street, I see no car. It's only after he revs the engine that I realise Petar has a motorbike. He gets on, helps me up. No words. Not even one. No more fucking words. We whiz around the town's empty roads, from Mitnica to Sajmište, and all the way to Adica, then back. I hold onto him for dear life, and beyond. Eventually, he delivers me home, all bright eyed and bushy tailed.

'Can I stay at yours?' I ask.

He shakes his head, smiling.

'But I want to!'

He grabs me around the waist and pulls me in for a short and sweet midnight kiss, then thunders off into the night.

I do, Petar. I definitely, positively do.

CHOREOGRAPHY FOR BEGINNERS

I loiter on our front lawn, loath to go in. The thought of my mother, all pregnant and angry, well it's more than I can take. Where the fuck am I supposed to go now. The night is warm. The sky's starry. I just wish I could go some place where I belong. What's wrong with that. What's wrong with me. Why wouldn't Petar take me with him.

I open the gate, ever so carefully. If you lift it off its hinges a little, it stops it from creaking like a right motherfuck.

'Good evening.'

Dad's sitting on an outside sofa in the middle of the yard, smoking. I thought he'd stopped. I used to want to put rainworms into his cigarette box, so he'd freak out and never smoke again. That was before I started sneaking the cigarettes out of the same box, three at the time, and smoking them behind the garage, one after another. Never liked the taste. But I do have the staying power of a psychopath. That's been said about me in the past, so it must be true.

'Why are you still up?' I ask Dad. 'Is everything alright?'

Not that I want to know. I am cross with this man.

Who does he think he is. A merry baby-maker. Wasn't Teodora enough to dissuade anyone from even thinking about fathering another child. Stupid, stupid man.

'Come here,' he says. Slurringly. Perhaps my dad is closer to Charles Bukowski than I imagined. 'Give your old man a hug.'

'You're not old,' I say. It's the truth. Iva's father, Buk's father, they're old men. Not Dad. 'Don't you dare say such a thing. Ever again.'

I give him a hug. His body feels skinny and small through his old yellow angora jumper. I love his yellow jumper. I chose it for him. We were in Paris, only the three of us because Teodora got chicken pox just before we were due to depart and had to stay with Mema, hurrah. From day one, Mum started to bug him to buy some French clothes. He was like, I already have everything I need. But Mum kept bugging. 'What's the point in visiting Paris,' she sighed. 'if you don't get at least one outfit out of it?'

Not for her, the world's finest museums and galleries, or the gothic architecture and breathtaking vista of wide open boulevards. All she wanted was to kit us all out in bourgeois gear everyone would envy back at home. I mean, we had our own seamstress and everything, you couldn't get more prêt-à-porter than that.

'Pick just one thing,' she sighed big. 'That's all I'm asking. Never mind whether you need it or not, just buy it.'

So in the end, Dad asked me to help him choose. I looked and looked, but couldn't see anything quite befitting my Daddy Darling. Until the very last day when I saw this fluffy yellow cloud floating around the window display at the Galleries Lafayette, and I said, 'This one, Daddy!' Mum laughed and laughed, until Dad said, 'Wonderful, Helena, you have a great eye for fashion!' He went in and bought the jumper there and then. I was so happy, I twirled around with joy, and had all these nice smelling old people smiling at me, clapping and giving me sweets from the tins they all seemed to carry around in their bags. Men, as well as women. The End.

'Oh, but I feel that way,' he says. 'I feel old, and decrepit, and alone.'

'Well snap out of it!' I shouted. Didn't mean to, my voice just rushed out all unruly. 'Mum told me. About, you know, the baby. So not exactly the time for you to go all doddery.'

He chuckles. Lucky him. I feel like I'm about to burst into tears. Like all's lost. 'Can you believe it?'

'I have to, don't I,' I say. 'Unless Mum has an abortion.'

There's silence. Eventually, he says, 'You don't mean it.'

I say nothing.

'It'll be alright, you'll see.'

'I know,' I say.

'We'll have to leave, of course... You do realise, don't you? It's not safe here any more.'

'Oh come on, Dad. People are exaggerating, as per usual.' But there's no conviction in my voice. 'I mean, where would we go?'

He sighs. 'I don't know. Down Dalmatia way... Your mother has family there.'

'You hate her family.'

'True. But it's not about me, is it.' He offers me a cigarette. I light one. It tastes so much better stolen. 'We may even have to go our own separate ways–'

'I'm going with you!'

'This may not be possible.'

'Make it possible.'

'Or safe.'

'Make it safe!'

'Oh, Helena… You're breaking my heart.'

'It'll mend!'

Oh, Helena…' Dad rubs his forehead. 'Can't you see I'm confused? What is a man supposed to do?'

'Stick with his older daughter.'

'Not if that would put her into danger,' he says. 'This much is clear, you must stay with Mum. Look after her for me.'

'No! She can have Teodora. And that's that! So stop upsetting me!' To show him just how upset I really am, I grab his glass and empty it. 'More!'

'You little opportunist,' he says. 'The bottle's behind the chair.'

I wake up with a plan. I'll make a list of the good things in my life. Then I'll make a list of things in my life that are not so good. I'll tear up each entry, put it into my old bowler hat. It used to belong to my granddad, Dad's father. He was a gentleman. And a scholar. Didn't like Mum very much. Anyway: I'll shake it all up, and each new morning I'll take a piece of paper out of the hat and read it out loud. Sometime it will be good news. Other times, it will be bad. But at least I will have it right there in front of me: it is not all bad. Some of it is good.

I sit on the kitchen floor, surrounded by pieces of paper. The hat is empty. Miko doesn't like the paper being strewn all over the floor. He likes to have order in his life. He's biting into it, chewing it up, spitting it out. At first, I try and stop him, but then I think what's the point. At least someone's having fun around here. The first bit of paper I pulled out was bad news. Fuck it, I thought, I'm gonna do it again. So I kept having another go, hoping for an instant cheer. Eventually, on my fifth attempt, I pulled out a piece that stated, "I am skinny". What sort of good news is that. I was always skinny. Which I've no doubt is better news than being fat, but I was always skinny. Nothing to write home about. Nothing to beat down the bad news with.

The news like, "I will be someone's sister again". Or, "Everyone's talking about the war". Or, "I am afraid". So fuck it. Stupid idea anyway. Miko may as well eat it.

Teodora comes back from her summer whoring tour looking all sun-kissed, wind-swept and fake.

'He was the most handsome of them all!' I overhear her saying to my pregnant mother. 'The other girls were so jealous!'

'Well,' my mum says. 'You are such a pretty girl. I'm not surprised to hear that boys fall over themselves to be with you.'

Teodora checks her reflection in the window, flicks

her bleached goldilocks about, eventually spots me standing on the other side. 'Ahhhhhh!' she shrills. Surprised the windowpane remains intact.

'What on earth, Teodora?' Mum looks cross. Good. 'Are you trying to give me a heart attack?'

'It's Helena! She scared me on purpose!'

'How old are you?' I walk in from the veranda. I'm hungry. Wonder if I should have any more of that cherry pie Mum made yesterday. Or shall I just go for a thickly buttered salami sandwich, perhaps with some of the last year's pickle. Or maybe a tomato. Hmm. 'Go fetch me a tomato from the garden.'

Teodora looks as if I've slapped her. 'Are you talking to me?'

'Yes. You. Go get, and make sure it's ripe. But not soft. I like my tomatoes nice and firm. But ripe. Okay? Now mush.'

She checks if Mum's looking, flashes me a middle finger.

'Mum,' I say. 'Afraid I have a crime to report.'

'Who's the baby now?' Teodora whines. Christ. She ain't no fun. Not even to tease, because she never gets anything. 'You are!'

'Talking of babies…' I start but the expression on Mum's face is so fierce it stops me dead in my vocal tracks.

Teodora, the vulture that she is, picks up on this. 'What?' she goes. 'You started, so you may as well finish it now.'

Oh yeah. Like that's going to work. Reminds me of boys who say their balls will shrivel and die in total agony if a girl doesn't finish them off. Could possibly

166

think of a few bigger turn-offs, but not right now. So Teodora doesn't know about Mum having a bun in the oven. Can't believe I just said that. Bun in the oven. Christ. I had better wash out my mouth with soap and water. Dirty words, true words. My mother is going to have a baby. There will be war. I am feeling lonely. I have been feeling lonely all my skinny little ass life.

Well I don't see why Teodora must be protected from knowing what's really going on around here. She should suffer too. 'Didn't Mum tell–'

'Shut up, Helena!' I have never heard Mum speak with such evil force before.

I think this baby must be some kind of a demon. 'Go to your room!'

Go to my room. Can't believe my ears. Teodora still has this vulturish, mustn't miss a trick look, but she also looks clearly delighted with Mum barking at the wrong daughter. Little cunt. And a big cunt. Fuck them both, I'm out of here.

SOCIALIST FEDERAL REPUBLIC OF
YUGOSLAVIA
Vukovar, Republic of Croatia
1991.

There are three kinds of calms in this world: calm
before the storm, calm in between storms, and calm
after the storm. Some people count the calm before
and the calm after the storm as one and the same, but
that is an illusion. For there is an unmistakable dip in
the energy field just before the fated event takes place,
and then there is a quivering vacuum that is left in its
aftermath. Two very different things. As my
thousand-year Balkan assignment approaches its
completion, I look back at my time here as a collection
of brief periods of peace arranged in between many
violent storms. I weathered them all, but more
notably, so did the Balkan peoples.

They come from afar, to test my ability to predict the
future, as well as their own ability to believe in what
I tell them. Little do they know that, as a truesayer, it
is my purpose on this earth to tell the truth – and so
help me God, that is what I do. Having spent
millennia amongst humans, observing them in life as

well as death, I have learnt never to underestimate the extent of their need to live a lie, and I adjust the conveyance of the truth accordingly. And they keep coming back. I have had no single free Sunday since March 1990, which is just over a year ago. Yes, I do give them the truth, but I never leave them with a stone in the pit of their stomach. I help them digest it, the best I can.

'Where are you from, my child?'

The woman sitting in the chair opposite me is young, no more than thirty years of age, and pretty, in that salt of the earth way admired by the more effeminate type of men. She arrived on my doorstep carrying a glass vase filled with brightly coloured plastic flowers and a huge box of chocolates with a dented corner.

'Hope you like the flowers, Baba Lepa. I made them myself, when I still worked at the ornamental flower department at the factory. Then one day they decided to move me to funeral and memorial services. Just like that. Nothing I could do about it, even though I hate it there.' She points at the chocolate box. 'I sat on it by mistake. Sorry. I don't seem to be able to concentrate any more, my life's become one calamity after another, total chaos – and I blame the local priest!' I watch her wring her large bony hands, carefully assembled on the top of the table. 'Priests are supposed to help weak and vulnerable women like myself, not curse and crucify them!'

I smile inwardly. Weak and vulnerable are hardly

the adjectives that spring to mind when I look at this young lady. The first thing I noticed about her was the heavyset square jaw that led the rest of her body into the room, from her broad angular shoulders to her wide fleshy feet. But it was not only her physical appearance that implied great vigour, there was something else about her, an unbridled quality that I suspected compelled her to act as a force of nature in human form – rarely a fortunate combination. 'What is your name?'

'Radmila Savić.' Radmila takes a sip of water I pulled out of the well only this morning. 'I must say, this is a very tasty glass of water. Cool and crisp.'

'Have you travelled far?'

'Southern Serbia, a small village near Leskovac.'

'Which one?'

'Jašunja. Not much of a village, really.' Radmila puckers up her plump lips into a coquettish pout. 'They say Jašunja men make the best lovers in the whole of Serbia, and I would be inclined to agree – not that I slept with every single one of them, of course.'

'Of course.' I look at the man standing to Radmila's left, with both his hands buried deep into the thick blond locks of her waist-long hair. Stark naked, his skin is dark grey and glistening with layers of milky sweat. Judging by the length of his white hair and yellowing fingernails, this man has spent far too long wandering around the afterlife. Every now and again, he rubs his fully erect penis against Radmila's breast and arm, but she does not notice this. To her, this man clearly is long dead and gone. 'I believe people of Jašunja are also blessed with two great monasteries.'

'So you heard of us?' Radmila seems none too pleased. 'Glad someone has. I hate it there, you know. Cursed be the village life, harsh in the winter, and even worse in the summer, when your blood comes alive and you feel like it's going to burst out of your veins if you don't do something… Anything!' Her eyes flood with anger. 'Anything at all!'

As it happens, not only have I heard of Jašunja, but I have also visited it on my mission to help move along one Sofia Romanova, who was perhaps my all-time favourite client. One of the lesser Romanovs, Sofia arrived at the Monastery of the Presentation of the Holy Mother of God in Jašunja in 1932, together with a dozen other blue-blooded Russian woman seeking safety. What they found was a derelict building with no livestock, an empty granary, and no bed. Still, they decided to stay, and make the best with what little they had. Sofia Romanova was the force behind their survival thus far, so it was only to be expected that she would take over the restoration project with the passion of a true tyrant. She drove the women, as well as herself, to work from dawn to dusk, relentless in her pursuit of recreating the semblance of their lost home, and within a year the place was transformed into a comfortable refuge for body and soul. Alas, once the crisis was over, Sofia took to her bed and remained there for days. At first, her sisters feared she would die, but as days turned into weeks and weeks turned into months, with Sofia still barking orders from what was supposed to be her deathbed, they began to pray that she would. Sofia, however, refused to expire just yet. 'I did not go through all that hardship in order to leave its fruit uneaten!'

Somebody had to do something – and this was where I came in, to assess the situation and act according to my findings. The moment I entered her bedroom, Sofia looked up at me and said, 'Go back where you came from, you old devil! There is nothing here for you, but a wasted journey.'

I smiled, for I could see her soul was already stood beside her defiant body, tapping its foot. 'Come on, Sofia Romanova, enough is enough. Even you must see this.'

'What do you mean, even me? Eh? Why are you talking to me as if I were slow?'

'Because you are,' I said. 'You are slow to catch up with the reality of your predicament.'

'You insolent woman – or whatever it is that you are.' She turned her head towards the window and pretended to stare at it for a while. I knew she was making her own assessment of the situation, weighing the pros and cons, covering all the angles. 'What is it that you are trying to tell me, eh? What is it I am supposedly not comprehending?'

'Your work here is done,' I said. 'And your resistance to moving on is threatening to reverse the good you have accomplished.'

'Nonsense!'

Our eyes locked. 'Sofia Romanova, it is time for you to go.'

Eventually, she lowered her eyes. 'Stop gawping

at me like a hungry vulture. I will go.' She then picked a hand bell and rang it until all the women lined up in front of her, in a various state of undress – for this was the middle of the night, after all.

'I want a duck egg. Soft boiled. A pinch of salt, no bread. I shall eat it, and after I have eaten it, I shall die. You may watch – in fact, I insist that you should.' She pointed her gnarly forefinger at me. 'In case this one gets up to no good.' The women exchanged puzzled glances, for they were not able to see me. 'What are you waiting for, my sisters? Do you not know that Death waits for no one!'

And indeed, she was right.

But I digress. Back in the here and now, in my role as a truesayer, I continue to entertain Radmila's story about the curse the old priest had allegedly put on her because he mistook her for a rapacious seductress of all the good men of Jašunja, which could not be further away from the truth. 'That's the thanks I get for being friendly and helpful to all folk, including the sick, and even crippled! When the widower Janko lost his right foot after it got caught up in one of his own bear traps, who do you reckon cooked his dinner every single night for over a month?'

'You?'

'Yes – me! Pardon my tone, Baba Lepa, but the whole situation's so unfair, it's making my blood boil! That randy old goat, the priest, he wanted me ever since I first bled. But I wouldn't go with him, the last thing I needed was the reputation of being a priest's mistress, no man would come near me again! So he decided that if he couldn't have me, no one could. I haven't had a man in almost six months, and counting! I beg of you, Baba Lepa, remove this awful jinx so I can go free!'

Never thought I would say this, but I shall miss humans once I am gone. 'There is no curse, my child. Or jinx. Or spell. You are already free.'

'Really?' Radmila looks disappointed. 'In that case, please tell me if it would be auspicious for me to pack my bags and start life from scratch some place new. Like Vukovar.'

I admire her elasticity. 'Why Vukovar?'

'Well, why not?' Says Radmila. 'I like this town already, but I'm going to like it even better once it's been liberated.'

'Liberated?'

'Once we get rid of the Croats, and other riffraff. There are plenty of good honest Serbian folk like myself, ready to move into their empty houses, take over the land, look after the livestock. That's what the priest said, anyway, and for once the old toad was right.'

I send Radmila on her way with a dropper bottle filled with nothing but my home-made cherry brandy, tell her to take a drop three times a day for thirty days, and obey the voice of her intuition. As she skips over the threshold, excited at the thought of all the fun she will be having with all the new men in her new life, her silent companion trails in her wake.

'Not so fast,' I say, then throw a lasso made out of a silky silver yarn, which closes neatly around his neck. He yelps in surprise, and tries to set himself free. 'You will need to leave that woman alone from now on, do you hear? In fact, you will need to leave, full stop, for it has gone way past your bedtime.'

Heart-broken lovers are the hardest to move on. Even if their love was one hundred per cent unrequited, they still fiercely cling onto the hopes and dreams they had woven whilst they were still alive. Radmila's secret admirer is no different.

'She told me she loved me,' he said, once he calmed down enough to accept the truth about his predicament. 'She told me she would be mine. I planned to take her away from the village, to Leskovac, or maybe even Niš. Away from her past, so we could start afresh, together.'

'Still,' I say. 'Hardly a reason to rub your privates against an unknowing woman.'

'My sincere apologies, Baba Lepa. I haven't felt like myself of late.' He touches the deep, purple-coloured track the noose had left around his neck. 'I remember the poppies the best. An entire field of big bright red poppies, and Radmila's body writhing under the body of another man... I would like to see the poppies again. Any chance you can put me back as I was? Please, Baba Lepa, please bring me back to life!'

Matija is a regular. She lives across the road, with her husband and two daughters, but originally hails from the gnarled backbone of Biokovo mountain in the Croatian South, believed by many to contain the heart and soul of the entire Croat nation.

Matija was only seven years old when she woke up next to the body of her dead mother. On her sixteenth birthday, her beloved brother Tomislav had stolen her from right under their father's nose, and took her with him to the more civilised North.

'You are not going to end up like Mother,' said Tomislav. 'Used and abused, in body and soul, until the merciful God took pity and freed her from her never-ending toils.'

Matija finished her education at Vukovar Gymnasium, then with a little help from Tomislav's friends in high places, she landed a job as a legal secretary at the local council. This is where she first met the young Serbian intellectual, Stefan, and the two of them fell in love. Stefan proposed within a year. Matija said yes, despite her brother's grave reservations.

'Stefan is a good man,' said Matija.

'I would never argue with that,' said Tomislav. 'But he is a Serb.'

'From a good family,' said Matija.

'Serbian family.'

'I'm not marrying them,' said Matija. 'I'm marrying Stefan.'

'You stubborn little mare! With your looks and your brains, you could've done this back in Imotski, and done much better for yourself than some piss-poor provincial university professor!' Tomislav took his sister's head in his hands so she had no choice but meet his eyes. 'Sister... I brought you here so you could better yourself, become an independent woman... See the world, savour it, develop your palate, no need to stick to the first flavour you taste! I beg of you, give up Stefan and come away with me, let's get the last train to Zagreb this very evening, and start afresh!'

But Matija shook her head free. 'No. Enough running, I'm staying put. Stefan is the man for me, and I hope you will see that one day, and I pray that you would.'

Tomislav had one last card left up his sleeve. 'What about your children?'

Matija's cheeks turned red. 'Please, brother, we have not– I mean, we do not–'

'I hope you realise that any children you may have with Stefan will be condemned to a life of confusion. Half-Croat and half-Serb, they'll have no identity to speak of, no side to turn to when this Yugoslavian utopia falls apart, as it surely will one day.'

Matija's eyes flashed with anger. She stood up, and said, 'Do not try and scare me, my brother. And you leave my unborn babies out of this, for they will be the true Yugoslavs, the true children of this land and its past, its present and, most importantly, its future.'

'Helena is driving me mad,' says Matija. 'One minute she's acting all sulky and depressed, the next minute she's storming the place like a whirlwind. If I ask her a question, no matter how trivial, she becomes so evasive I start suspecting the worst, like maybe a marijuana addiction, or she may give me one of her super-precocious answers, designed to make me feel like the stupidest woman on earth. I swear she's winding me up on purpose. She must be, Baba Lepa, else why would she be able to press practically every single button I've got?'

Having had the pleasure of meeting young Helena, and taking into consideration my ability to see through the fabric of illusion that is space, time and matter, I feel confident when I say, 'No need to worry. Any differences that exist between Helena and yourself will soon become the thing of the past.'

Matija visibly relaxes. 'Oh, good.'

'But tell me, my child, what really brings you here?'

She wrings her hands, in a far less theatrical fashion than Miss Savić: Matija keeps hers neatly huddled on top of her lap, and the only reason I get to see her distress is because it is not only the metaphysical materials I am able to see through, but also the more mundane ones, such are kitchen tables, impenetrable fortress' walls and people's flesh, to name but a few.

'It's this war business,' she eventually offers. 'I don't have anyone to talk about it with, not even at home – especially not at home. My husband is busy trying to persuade the academic administration at the university that he is not a potential political liability. My friends, well, they've been keeping to themselves lately... So the thoughts keep sloshing around in my head, the terrifying ones drowning out the more sensible insights. I want to believe it is all a rumour, a conspiracy plot devised to give our politicians a flicker of consequence, but even if that were true, the masses seem to have fallen for it. People are scared. I'm scared. The only person who doesn't seem at all affected by this is Helena. She is still behaving as if none of this matter, as if she's above it all. I do not understand that girl. My younger daughter, Teodora, she just gets on with it, no trouble at all. Helena despises her, of course, as I believe she despises me, and everyone else who doesn't happen to be her favourite writer, or of course her Daddy.' Matija shrugs. 'I don't think she's even kissed a boy yet, except for that imaginary friend of hers, Jimmy, whom she used to drag around with her everywhere she went from the age of two until she started school. She used to say that he lived inside the hall mirror, and she kept kissing that mirror until I got tired of wiping off the marks, and I told her to stop, told her that Jimmy doesn't exist, and never did. I will never forget the look she had given me.' Matija shudders. 'Such a strange girl. I do not understand her at all.'

'Matija,' I say. 'Do you really believe that there is war is coming?'

'What else am I to believe? People are tired of the status quo. Funny thing, though, Vukovar is buzzing with this vibrant new energy; everyone seems so alive. The colour, long faded out of people's lives, has suddenly returned. Strikes me as a sad paradox, to remember how to live just as death approaches.'

I allow for her words to drift out through the wide-open window, before asking, 'What will you do?'

'I don't know,' says Matija. 'But I feel we'd better make a decision before someone makes it for us.' I pour water into her glass, she takes a little sip. 'Thank you. Hard to believe there's no sugar in this water, it tastes so sweet.'

I fetch a crystal pot from the closet and place it in front of my guest, together with a small silver spoon.

'Rose petal jelly, made with pink roses only. Journeys directly to your heart.'

Matija helps herself. 'Delightful.'

I wholeheartedly agree. 'Your husband, he must have some ideas, no?'

'I feel his loyalties are somewhat divided.' She pauses for a moment. 'No, not divided – confused. Perhaps my brother was right when he warned me not to marry a Serb. Mixed marriages are not best placed to survive civil wars.'

'And yet they do,' I say. 'All the time, all over the world.'

Matija looks up at me. 'Do they?'

'Oh yes. A lot of people still urge sticking to your own clan when it comes to procreation, because they are worried about diluting their bloodline out of existence. But nature adores alchemy. Where do you think human evolution would be were it not for the mixed marriages stirring up the gene pool? Insistence on keeping things pure puts the entire race in danger of extinction. The only way to progress is through crossbreeding: nature knows this, and therefore conspires to protect its best assets – and this, my dear Matija, includes you and your husband, and especially your children, both born and unborn.'

Matija places her hands on her belly. 'You know?'

'It is my job. Congratulations.'

'But – a newborn? At time like this?'

'What is more sacred than bringing a new life into the world governed by death? No need to be concerned: your child will be blessed.'

Matija lets out a frustrated little sigh. 'I'm grateful

for your kind words, I really am, but I need a more tangible insight – I need you to tell me how to ensure that we all survive what's coming without breaking up our family, or getting killed in the process. I need you to tell me, because I have lost faith in my ability to work this one out. I spent many a wakeful night lying motionless next to my husband, praying for sleep to come, praying for a dream to visit me and bring the right answer. And the following morning, I would sleepwalk through yet another long and barren day, looking for a sign, hoping to find a solution amongst the mundane, but all I ever seem to accomplish is further confusion. I'm lost, so lost, and I beg of you, Baba Lepa, tell me what to do.' She stares at me for a few moments. I hold her gaze, but remain quiet. We sit in silence for a while, until eventually Matija clears her throat, and says, 'I think we should all go South, to Dalmatia... Stay at my brother's holiday house on the island of Hvar, don't suppose there will be much fighting there. The islanders have always been most welcoming to Stefan in the past. And, unlike Vukovar, Hvar is hardly known for being a nationalistic epicentre of Croatia. What do you think, Baba Lepa? Does this sound like a good plan to you?'

A calm before the storm has reached its lowermost point. The inhabitants of Vukovar have fallen still and silent, watching the odd flash of lightning breaking up the horizon, listening out for a distant rumble of thunder, counting the breathless seconds in between.

The storm is coming.

It is time for me to leave.

THE GENTLE ART OF PERSUASION

But where shall I go. I stand in the middle of an empty pavement. I look up, I see the blue sky, unravelling forever more. I look down, see my feet. Green flip-flops. Grey paving stones. I look left, the street disappears in the summer's day haze. Right, the poplar trees murmur something that I feel bears no translating.

I cross the road. Wish I wasn't wearing the flip-flops. I never usually do. What's up with me these days. Not knowing where I'm going, and wearing totally wrong footwear for it. I find myself in front of Baba Lepa's black iron gates. There's no bell. Or a knocker. Or a letter box. It's like an impenetrable barrier between two worlds. I bang on it, half-heartedly. Don't want to hurt my hand. Or attract too much attention. I bang again. No answer. No one's home. I kick it, but again, neither my heart nor my toes are really in it. Kicking like a girl, what's the point. No one's going to hear that. Or take any notice. I know I wouldn't.

I walk away, dragging my feet just in case the gates suddenly open to let me in. But the last minute pardon never happens when you expect it to. Ask any former death row inmate. So I slip onto a dirt track leading to Dola. I hope the numerous snakes who no doubt live around here are having a nice long siesta right about now. Although, aren't they at their most agile in hot weather. And go all frozen in the winter. The thought of their pointy faces, their sharp teeth, their soulless eyes. I stop dead in my tracks. For real this time. The fear paralyses me for a second. Wish I wore my Dr Martens.

I stand there, ankle deep in yellow dust, afraid to move in any direction whatsoever. No place safe enough, no direction that pulls. I look around for clues. Dry blades of grass, and their unnerving, fragmented low whisper. Balding mounds of earth, with dolls' arms, old shoes, washing machine drums and umbrella wires randomly poking out all over the place. Wild fruit trees, scattered about the place, watching over this unloved kingdom like a skeleton army. Crows, poking about in someone's long neglected allotment, making sure no good seed's left behind in this earth, to maybe grow and turn into something bigger and better – but not even remotely useful to your average crow. A man, sitting behind a trunk that used to belong to the linden tree that got struck down by lightning when I was about five. He spots me back, and gets to his feet. He looks familiar, but then again things tend to do that a lot when you live in one of the world's last remaining backwaters where nothing moves and everyone's stuck neck-deep in mud.

'Hi,' he says.

'Hi.'

'Bit hot today.'

Talking weather. This is even worse than a snake attack. Except maybe for that Indiana Jones snake attack, when he fell into that Egyptian tomb. Or was he thrown in. By a Nazi. 'Yes, it is a bit hot, for, er, a summer's day.'

'I agree.'

I mess up a bit of dust in front of me with a tip of my badly dressed toes. Draw little circles, and shit. The next minute, the guy is doing the same. Except he's wearing a pair of tr–trrr–trrra–TRAINERS. Aghh. Now I have to wash out my brain with soap and water. And what's up with this mirror shit, is he a mime or something.

'Soo…' I hear myself say. 'What are you doing here?'

'Well…' He looks around, furtively (as they would no doubt say in a badly written book). Must be because this derelict corner of our demi-world is full of spies who get an extra-special hard-on just by listening to what losers like him have to say. 'I'm waiting for my girlfriend.' He points at one of the dirt mounds. 'She's hiding over there.'

'Why?'

'I'm guessing she's upset. With me.'

'What did you do to her?'

'Nothing!'

'So why is she upset with you then?'

He shrugs. 'All I know is, one minute we were walking down to my place, laughing and joking, then the next minute, she freaks out and runs off into Dola.' He scratches the back of his head. 'Could be the seven large whiskies she had in town... I hate it when she drinks dark spirits.'

'Yeah, but you said she was upset with you.'

He actually thinks about this. What fun. 'Okay – not upset. More like sulking.'

Well of course she is. Women sulk. Men bring in meat. Women sulk. Men work the land. Women sulk. Men drink sake. Women? They make a molehill into a mountain, only so they can sulk behind it. Grr-arghh. Does this make me a feminist. I notice the guy's staring at me in that enthusiastically-concerned sort of way, which just happens to be one of my favourite pet-hates. 'What?'

'Did you just growl a little?'

I shrug. 'Might've done. It's the heat. Grr. Arghh.'

He looks relieved. 'Yes. Turns you into an animal, it does. Grr indeed.'

I should leave. But I don't. Nowhere to go, see. 'Tell me more about your girlfriend. Do you, like, love her, and stuff?'

'With all my heart.' Ew. I think it, but what I feel is pure bile-green envy.

Is bile even green. Double ew. 'But I won't lie to you, I don't understand her. One moment she's all happy and nice to me, the next – boom!'

'Just like that?'

He puts both hands on his heart. 'I swear. I'd never do anything to provoke her.'

Well no wonder she's upset. 'Moody times, these, people are freaking out all over the place.'

'Tell me about it.' He offers his hand. 'I'm Nikola, by the way.'

'Helena.'

We shake on it. He has a nice firm shake, no sweat at all. I allow him another glance. He's not bad looking, I'll give him that. I'm starting to feel a pulsating kind of itch in the frilly pink knickers I stole from Teodora. I seem to have lost my entire knicker stash. Wonder what could've happened to it.

'We are supposed to go away this afternoon,' he says. 'I have a house on Cres, you know – Northern Adriatic, and I thought it would be nice for both of us to get away from it all.'

My ears prick up. 'Cres?'

'Yeah. At the edge of the town, peace and quiet, just the way I like it. In actual fact, I'd love to live there, full-time like, but...' He glances back towards the girlfriend-mound. 'Not without Elena.'

'Elena?'

'My girlfriend,' says Nikola.

What a stupid name. 'But why?'

'Why what?'

'Why would you forsake the place you love for a moody bit of skirt?' Well that was a long sentence. But this is how you have to speak to these people. Spell it all out.

'I don't know what that means,' says Nikola.

And still it's not enough. I sigh. 'Why don't you go without her?'

'Are you joking?' He stares at me. 'I would feel like I had a limb missing.'

'Right.' I feel even more envious. And a little cross. Silly girl, not jumping at the opportunity to get the fuck out of here. To this amazing place where there're hardly any people. With a guy so badly besotted, she could wrap him around her little finger like a piece of old chewing gum. 'So why won't she come?'

'Doesn't want to leave her family behind. Especially her sister.'

My jaw drops so low it hurts. 'You're kidding, right?'

Nikola shakes his head. 'Not at all.'

'Is your girlfriend one of those people who never travel?' We've all heard those stories. 'Who never wander further than their street corner, because they're happy where they are?'

'You mean like a hermit?'

Well that sure was a big word. 'Yeah, something just like that.'

'I suppose she is a little bit like a hermit,' says Nikola. 'Except she likes to party.'

A partying hermit. 'I see.'

'Hey,' he then says. 'Look who's coming to join us.'

I turn around. First impressions are surprisingly favourable. Whilst Nikola seems full of rude health and wears tr–trr–oh fuck it, the girl walking gingerly towards us looks freshly risen from the dead. Document-white, bloodless skin. Jet black hair, an obvious slapdash home-dye. Ruby red lips, smudged. Mascara running all the way down her chin. Small black lacy dress, hardly covering her ass – I'm guessing a childhood item. Big boots, no laces. Not sure if they are Dr Martens, but they look cool is all that matters. Elena looks like a girl who doesn't really want to live, is petrified of growing up, but doesn't want to die, either. A little vampire.

'Fuck,' she goes. 'I feel like shit.' She stumbles for no apparent reason and goes down, but Nikola catches her just before she hits the ground. 'Arghhh! Get off!' He lets her go, rolls his eyes at me. Like we know each another or something. Elena gives me a mean look. 'Who the fuck is she? And what the fuck's she doing here?'

'How rude,' I say. 'I was here before you.'

'Errr,' goes Nikola. 'That's not entirely true, is it now?'

'You're only travelling through this place.' I am aware I sound like the I Ching, but for some reason I can't stop myself. 'I, on the other hand, was born here.'

Elena's eyes grow meaner still. 'What, in Dola?'

I can see how I walked straight into this one. I drop all pretence of Tao. 'What's your problem?'

She makes her voice small and baby like, 'What's your problem?'

'Now, now, Elena,' says Nikola. 'Helena here is a friend.'

'Helena, is it?' says Elena. 'What a stupid name.'

Right. This bitch is starting to piss me off. 'Listen you little–'

'How about we all have a drink together,' says Nikola. 'Start afresh, what do you say?'

Elena and I drop our weapons like two perfectly synchronised robo-warriors.

'We have drink?' she goes.

'A few bottles of wine…' Nikola gives her a meaningful look. 'You know… The wine?'

'Oh, right.' Elena turns to me. 'I stole a few bottles of wine from my granny. She'll never drink it, because she's like, dying and stuff.'

'Don't be saying stuff like that about baka Mara,' says Nikola. 'She's the kindest lady I've ever met.'

'Why don't you go marry her if you love her so much?' says Elena. 'But first, go fetch our stuff, and hurry the fuck up.'

'Your wish…' Nikola buggers off.

Elena and I find a soft grassy spot nested in between three plum trees, and sit down in a shade.

'Sorry I was ratty with you,' she says. 'Bloody daytime naps, they do my head in.'

'You were asleep?'

'A-ha. Why? What did that moron tell you I was doing?'

'Thinking.' I don't know why I lie here, but I do. 'About Cres.'

Elena frowns. 'He told you about Cres?'

'Yeah. He wants you to come along, says it would be meaningless without you.' I'm starting to feel like a marriage counsellor. The price you have to pay for a few drinks. And a spot of time-killing. 'Plus I think he may be worried about being caught up in this war they're all talking about…'

Elena stares at me with her gold-freckled moss green eyes. Christ. Am I a lesbian now. 'You don't believe the war is really coming, do you?'

I think about it. Instead of simply batting it back. I think about it. This girl must have some magic power over me. 'No. The whole thing, it's just too, I don't know, idle? And narrow-minded, and lazy. People are bored, their lives feel empty, and the talk of war makes for easy entertainment.'

Elena perks up. 'I so agree with you! I mean, where's the enemy? Where are the Nazis? Or are we meant to have neighbour on neighbour action – what, here in Vukovar? Give me a break! Can you even imagine, like, your dad shooting some old man next door, who once upon a time gave him sweets and bounced him on his knee, just because he's, oh I don't know, a Muslim?'

I see how it has to be a Muslim. Muslims make for easy targets, especially around the southern Pannonia Plain, which has been appropriated by Serbs and Croats for the last zillion years, bar the odd century of rude interruption by the Ottoman and Habsburg Empires. I remember my dad helping my thick sister with her history homework once, and saying, 'Yugoslav Muslims aren't proper Muslims, you know. They used to be Slavs, just like us, but then along came the mighty Turk who bribed and maimed them into changing their faith. And a man without faith is a man without destiny. I feel sorry for them.'

Nothing's ever forgotten around here. Let alone forgiven. No slight ever allowed to go to waste. It runs through our collective veins, this unforgiving streak. We're all born with it, even I, except I try and dilute mine as much as possible with alcohol and other trusty blood thinners, like great literature, and film, and a few dreams of escape of my very own making. And most importantly, I don't go around hating Muslims. People in general, however, now that's another story.

'You're dead right, you know,' I say. 'Never gonna happen.'

190

'Exactly!' Elena is looking at me like I bet she never looked at Nikola, not even if he managed to give her the biggest orgasm of her life, which frankly I can't see ever happening, not with his pedestrian brain. But I'm far too old and wise to fall for those eyes. Seen it all before, I have: so a person stumbles into your life, looking all sparkly, and filled with promise that they may be The One – the unique one, the magical one, the righteous one; in short, the one you wouldn't have to hide your own genius from. For theirs would be almost as great and mighty, soaring free; together you would fly high above the rest. But then, suddenly and for no apparent reason, they would change. Just like Iva changed.

Iva and I were so close people would actually go blind to our evident physical distinction and believe us to be twin sisters. Oh how I adored the exclusive feel of our friendship, how I loved the fact we hardly even had to talk in order to get one another. We read each other's thoughts without a moment of doubt or hesitation; we celebrated each other's idiosyncrasies; we indulged each other's imagination by letting it run wild, by running wild with it. We soared together, Iva and I, at least for a while. Before she started to long to get back to earth, and her wings grew so tired she felt she had no choice but to have them clipped.

I wish Iva was dead. Not just deadened by human aspiration, blinded by fool's gold, but for real, dead and buried into the soft Slavonian soil. I reckon I could cope with that, and who knows, maybe I could even cry for her a little. Melt this sore spot in the middle of my chest that grew bigger in Iva's wake.

And it's still growing, I know it is. I have a bad feeling about this. Like I'm going to die. Like I should talk to someone about it. Except, I have no one to talk to. Baba Lepa is gone. I don't want to see no doctor. My parents are running scared not to mention pregnant, and besides they let me down a long time ago, when they brought Teodora into my oh so perfect world and ruined it forever. Can't talk to Iva, Jovan's gone, too, and as for all those brilliant friends I have not met yet, well I feel it's too late for that now.

I have no one.

I look at the little vampire girl sitting on the dirt mound, chatting shit, smoking fags, lost in space. Despite her Western clothes, and her dirty mouth, and her whiskies at noon, she doesn't even know she has wings, let alone how to use them. Hanging around with Nikola will hardly help her find them. Because Nikola is a wing-clipper. Dirt-dweller. Dust-kicker. Line-plodder. A regular guy, for short. She kind of knows this, bet that's why she won't come away with him. Part of her still wants to fly. I wonder how long would it take for her to stop caring altogether. 'So, do you think you may change your mind? About Cres?'

'Oh, I don't know, I don't like being pushed into doing things.' Elena suddenly looks like a fox with a plan. 'I don't like having my wings clipped, before I even tried them for size.' Well fuck me never. Is everyone around here a mind reading spy. 'You know what I mean?'

All I manage is a nod.

'I want to go to London.' She's playing with

strands of her thickly layered black locks. There's something about Elena. Unnerving. One minute she tells you to fuck off, the next minute she's purring. She reminds me of someone, must be a character from a book, or a movie. 'My dad has friends there. He says the major perk of any civil war is a chance to flee to the West, never to return.'

'But how?'

'You buy a plane ticket to any Western country you like, and once you hit their soil, and the Immigration's all, like, what the fuck are you doing trying to infiltrate our land of plenty, you pull the war card and watch all the blood drain out of their faces.' Elena glances at Nikola, who's busy carting a black leather rucksack, a battered red suitcase, a giant straw hat and a yellow spacehopper. 'They give you a leave to remain, which is basically your ticket to the citizenship, mission accomplished.'

'But what if they don't?'

'They have to, by law,' says Elena. 'It's called the Aliens Act, something like that, so you get to be an alien for a while, cool or what?'

Hate to admit, but yes, it's definitely cool.

'So that's why I have to stay put,' she then says. 'Vukovar may be a place that God forgot, but Cres – I don't think God's ever bothered finding in the first place.'

I never saw this coming. Calm, calculating, and nobody's fool, either. I am feeling slightly crushed by my misjudgement of Elena, because I pride myself on being a sound judge of human character, and I believe quite rightly so.

'Do you think you could help?' Nikola shouts over. 'Anyone? My hands are full!'

'Put the hat on!' Elena shouts back. 'It will set you free!'

'Funny!' He arrives huffing and puffing, just like a real boy. Or have I got my fairy tales well and truly scrambled. 'Seriously, you guys, I could've done with some help.'

Elena leans over and kisses his sweaty brow. I find myself:

a) looking away,

b) feeling envious, and

c) wanting to scratch the aforementioned knicker-itch real bad. I am not exactly head over heels to discover I have an unpredictable pussy. Where's the manual for that eh.

We take turns swigging from a bottle. Then another. The black rucksack keeps on delivering. Booze, but also the hard-boiled sweets old people seem to be so fond of, despite the clear and present danger of choking. And glazed honey biscuits. And an antique bird cage.

'Isn't it pretty?' says Elena, holding it up against the velvety afternoon rays. 'Perfect place for my feather collection.'

Turns out Elena was a proper little thief who didn't seem able to help herself when it came to appropriating other people's things.

'But only if I like really need it. And if they have plenty. And it goes without saying that I would never steal another's girl man, that's just too second-hand shop creepy.' Elena smiles like a Cheshire cat.

Honour amongst thieves, I get that. Can't get this girl, though. 'So where's your boyfriend, Elena?' She frowns. 'Wait a minute, that's me! H-elena. So, where's your boyfriend, Hhhhelena?'

'I don't have a boyfriend.'

'Buuuull-shiiiit,' goes Elena. 'Right, Nikola? Total bullshit, we don't believe a word she says!'

'I believe her,' says Nikola. 'I had no girlfriend for years, until I met you.'

'Please don't tell me that,' says Elena. 'Oi! Girl with a funny name! Spill!'

'It's true,' I say. 'No boy. No friend.'

'Really really? Bummer.' She stands up and drags me to my feet. Very strong, she is, for such a small thing. 'Let's dance!'

She pulls me close, starts singing and twirling me around. 'Stand by Your Man'. Her English says she's done this before. So we dance. And prance. We never quite fly, but it's fun. Later on, Nikola makes a fire. We dance around it, holding hands and pretending we're the champions of the world.

I open my eyes. The fire's almost out, the dawn on its way in. My head's resting on Nikola's left shoulder, Elena's on his right. I peel away and move closer to the fire, poke it about with random sticks in the hope of reviving it. I light a cigarette, it tastes rough. I pick up a lemon sweet from the ground, blow off the dirt, pop it into my mouth. Better. I lift my head up towards the East, then just like one of the old people who would never learn, almost choke on my sweet.

The sky has dropped its baby blue guise, and it's

bursting out in carmine red, in scarlet red, in fresh wound red, in as red as can be. My eye is confused, I rub it hard, then I rub my other eye. I look up again, but the horizon is still drowning in red; the waves of red are galloping towards me, casting jittery shadows across the land, drowning the earth, sucking out all the air. Once it's hit the zenith, the red forms into a huge pregnant belly; I watch it grow and grow until the skin breaks and releases zillions of malignant raindrops. I dive under a plum tree and I cover my head with my hands the best I can, so the sky cannot touch my head red, which I know would be fatal. A giant raindrop explodes somewhere in the lower part of Dola to my left. I crawl over, just in time to catch the sight of the last filaments of the red sky disappearing off into the earth, leaving behind a perfectly spherical crater. Suddenly, I know that the red sky is force-feeding the earth its consciousness, turning every living organism on earth into a toy-soldier under the command of the murderous, shattering red sky. Must tell Elena and Nikola. I crawl back over to the camp, and see the two of them, still sprawled on the floor, still asleep. 'Please God, don't let the red touch their heads!' I plead, then remember that God is no more, and besides I never did believe that he ever was.

I stare at Elena and Nikola, so beautiful, so peaceful, their pale little faces splattered red, dreamlike it seems, except I know a death mask when I see one.

So I collapse onto my knees and cry. I cry for them, I cry for myself, I cry for my pregnant mother, I cry for

Berlin and I cry for Vukovar. I rub my face with a handful of dust, I make mud with my tears.

'What's up with you?'

I look up and see dead Elena, sitting up straight, inspecting the bottom of a wine bottle. Shit, she must've been turned, taken apart and put together again, folded and unfolded to suit a malevolent new purpose. Behind her, Nikola's slowly rising, evolving into a new man, which may not be a bad thing. Still, I give out an ear-splitting scream, scramble up and run for my life. My bare feet fly over the clumps of grass and gnarly old roots, I leave only dust in my wake. I may even escape. I may be the one who got away. I may live. I may–

Something hits the back of my legs; I hit the ground so hard I actually see stars, silver and gold little beauties, flickering around my peripheral vision. I also bite into the fleshy part inside my own mouth and draw out about half a litre of blood. I hear someone laugh. Seriously. What sort of a person laughs at the time like this. I look up, see Baba Lepa, leaning against the chimney, peeling a large orange, her shiny black wings stretched out to her sides. I believe she's wearing a pair of black and white stripy tights that look suspiciously like the ones I lost, but I wouldn't quite dare swear on it in the court of law.

Someone whispers into my ear, 'Sorry!' It looks like I have Nikola on top of me, and not in a good way. I open my mouth to a) protest, and b) spit out a tooth or, fingers crossed, a pebble that's rolling around my mouth, but he presses his hand across the said orifice. Again, not in a good way. 'Listen!'

I listen, but can't hear anything at first, except for the sound of Nikola's over-the-top breathing. Wish he would stop already. Like Baba Lepa, who thank fuck is no longer laughing. And then it comes – the sound of distant thunder. Just when I thought the storm was over. I shake Nikola off, just enough so I can lift my head and peep over a scraggy hedge that stands between us and the road.

Right.

My eyes are clearly having a ball fucking with me today.

I stare at a line of the Yugoslav People's Army tanks negotiating their way towards Petrovci. I start counting. Automatically. Until I reach the number thirteen. And realise that counting them won't change the fact that there are tanks crawling up the street I grew up on. Still, the thought doesn't quite register, but buzzes around my head like an empty speech bubble I'd love to burst were I only allowed to move.

I risk a quick glance towards Baba Lepa. But there's no one on the roof. Even the sky has returned to its pale dawn lull. Like nothing weird had ever happened. I feel edgy, and it's not just the tanks. In actual fact, I doubt that I'm feeling the tanks at all. But I do feel kind of crushed about freaking out in front of these two complete strangers. I don't know why. Like, who cares. Besides, what are they going to do, tell the entire town. Tell everyone how Helena sees dead people walking underneath the red skies. What else is new.

Elena creeps up to my left.

'Mother fuck,' she whispers.

'Will you be coming to Cres now?' asks Nikola.

'I think I could be persuaded.'

'I dreamt of the red sky,' I say. 'It was a very vivid dream.'

'Hate vivid dreams.' Elena passes me a bottle of wine. I drink as much as one breath would allow.

'Red sky in the morning,' says Nikola. 'Shepherd's warning.'

What a strange thing to say.

EVE OF DESTRUCTION

I'm crouching on the first step leading to our cellar, sharing a chicken leg with Miko. We are hiding from the rest of the household, and have successfully done so for the last two days. He's purring so loud I'm certain someone will hear us, find us and make us do something we don't want to do.

'Shush, you beast,' I tell Miko. 'Shush.'

Which makes him drone even louder. I consider bribing him with the chicken bone, try to remember which animal isn't allowed to eat it, a dog or a cat. Most likely a dog. Too stupid to even chew. I give the bone to Miko. Don't think today's his day to die. He pounces on it like a motherfucking lion, but continues to purr. I smile. He's such a cool cat.

Today's Thursday. Elena and Nikola are finally leaving for Cres tonight. They've invited me to a party. Don't recall the last time someone's invited me to a party. Not that I would've gone.

'It's a Fuck You Goodbye party,' said Elena. 'It doesn't mean I'm gonna fuck everyone goodbye, okay Nikola, it's more like, we're off, so fuck you all kind of a party.'

'Oh,' I said. 'Can't wait.'

'It's mostly for Nikola's friends, guys from the band, his work colleagues, you know... So please come keep me company!'

I said I was going and so I'll go. Besides, it's much easier to avoid your parents if you're hiding some place other than own sweet home.

I leave Miko to it and stealth it up the stairs into my room. It's cool and dark in there, so I crawl under the covers for a little pre-party nap.

'Where were you?'

I jump out of my skin. Literally. I leave my body behind. 'Get out of my room, you filthy beast!'

But instead of following my instructions, Teodora walks right up to me, 'Where the fuck were you, you selfish cunt?'

Teodora's use of a c-word shocks me to the spot. 'What did you just call me?'

'Do you think Mum and Dad haven't got enough on their plates, without having to worry about Helena's wellbeing, Helena's whereabouts, Helena's past, Helena's present, Helena's flipping future!'

'I want you to leave my room. I won't tell you again. So...' I want to laugh, really, but I can't. She'll never take me seriously then, and I need her to leave me alone. 'Consider yourself well and truly warned.'

'Oh really? And what are you going to do if I don't? Bore me to death by reading from one of your precious volumes, let me see...' Teodora grabs the first book from the shelf, flips it open. 'But our love it was stronger by far than the love of those who were older than we, of many far wiser than we–'

I snatch the book out of her illiterate hands. 'Fuck off!' I stand in front of the bookshelf, my arms open wide. 'You come near my books again, and I'll–'

'You'll what? What, exactly, are you going to do? Run away? Because that's all you know how to do, run away, like a bloody coward.'

'That's not true… I almost never run away.'

Teodora stares at me in what appears to be an honest case of disbelief. 'Are you even for real?' Yep. It's disbelief. 'What is wrong with you?'

All I can think is that I asked her to leave, I even issued her with the last warning, and she's still standing here. Shouting at me. What am I supposed to do now. 'I think not. I think, er, it's more a case of what's wrong with you.'

This is where she swings out and lands a resounding slap across my face.

Damn.

What's with all the violence.

I am kicking every pebble I can find alongside the path. I jump up and down. I flail my arms around like windmill blades. I'd love to scream, but wouldn't like to attract any unwanted attention. If there is such a thing as wanted attention. Only from God, I reckon. I reckon it would be good to get God to appear on this abandoned, dead-end rail track that coils around Vukovar like a sleeping serpent. I guess it would be cool to get God's attention, for once. 'You sort it out, God all mighty, you take care of this shit!' I can't imagine anyone sorting out anything right now, though. Not even God. Nobody can undo what hasn't been done in the first place. Nobody can resurrect the life that cannot, or will not, be lived.

The rail track drops me off near Nikola's house. Not a complete dead end after all. Precious thing, this battered old rail track. It circumnavigates you right out of the town centre, all you need to do is hop on and off as you please. A lonely enough route to take on those days when the very thought of people makes me want to pee myself with terror. And when I say terror, I don't mean fear. I'm not afraid of people. Of what they might do to me. I don't really care about that. When I say terror, I'm talking about the idea of their lives superimposing upon mine. The very thought has the power to take my breath away. Or make me run for the loo. Or both.

Yeah. I much prefer to trudge the good old rail track, then take the dubious luxury of a quicker route. With an exception of an odd freight train, or a stray, of both canine and human kind, nothing threatens to jump at me out of the blue, overwhelm me with its horrific petty presence.

The sound of heavy-metal rock hits me like a hammer. Not a sledge hammer, but that annoying kind that forever keeps missing the nail. I must be very close to Nikola's house. I feel my stomach starting to churn. Nervous, are we. Haven't had a chance to sneak no liquor back home. Not after that savage attack from Teodora. I tore out of there like a bat out of hell. She tried to stop me, held onto my sleeve. Think she was crying, too. What the fuck has she got to cry about, the silly cunt. That's right – it is she who's a cunt. Not me. And I wish she was dead, dead, dead.

Violence doesn't exactly do wonders for a girl's self-esteem. First that crazy policeman, then my own mother, followed by the murderous red sky, tanks – and now Teodora. Have I forgotten anyone. Come on, people, make love not war. I linger in front of Nikola's gate, glancing up and down the street, wondering if the better opportunity awaits just around the next corner. If only I had a car, and knew how to drive it. I swear, I would just get in and drive off, and never stop driving until I got to some faraway place that felt safe enough for me to stay. I want to go home. That's all I ever wanted. How fucking hard can it be. I just want to go home. God! Fucker.

The sound of a motorbike pulling up on the front lawn brings me snap out of my bastard reverie. I turn to look, and surprise surprise, it's someone I know. That guy I met the other night at Buk's.

Petar. I feel hot under my invisible collar. How embarrassing, to have feelings. I feel my face turning red, I hope and sort of pray it doesn't show. He's not alone. A girl hops off the back, takes off the helmet, does the hair-ad thing, yanks the hotpants-wedgie out of her lovely ass, pouts for no reason. Petar smiles a little smile.

I feel crazy jealous. How weird. Altogether now: calm the fuck down. Let's try and keep it casual, okay.

'Thanks for the lift, babes.' The girl throws both arms around Petar's neck, presses herself against his leg, then pushes her tongue down his ear. The strange thing is, she's looking at me all the while. I'm not sure if this is supposed to make me want to hit her or fuck her. All I know that both options leave me feeling flat. 'Laters…'

I catch a whiff of Charlie eau de toilette as she walks on by. I used to spray this all over my dolls before they were due for an execution. Nothing unleashes a memory quite like a cheaply disguised BO.

'What are you doing here?' asks Petar. 'It's way past your bedtime.'

'I'm living a Proustian Moment,' I say. Good thing I don't mind sounding pompous. 'Your girlfriend's perfume was definitely a blast from the past.'

'You mean my sister?'

'Huh?'

'Sofija's my sister,' he says. 'Not my girlfriend.'

'Oh. Right.'

'She likes to provoke.' Petar takes my hand and places it under his arm. 'She loves the attention.'

'But she licked you,' I say.

'She never!'

'Yes, she did,' I say. 'I saw her.'

Petar laughs. 'And where's your evidence?'

I want to slap myself right now. Me, of all people, suddenly coming over all earnest. Not to mention a prude. 'Fuck off.' But I say this more to myself, than Petar.

'I'm only messing with you.' He leans into my head space, sticks his tongue into my ear. It sends an electric shock down every existing neural pathway in my body, before creating a few brand new ones. 'How does it feel?'

'It feels like being slobbered all over by a redneck,' I say. 'Don't ever do that again, you possum-eating, inbred hick.'

'You want me,' he says. 'Admit it.'

'I so do not.'

'Maybe tonight's your lucky night.' Petar opens the gate for me. 'You just never know.'

Too many people, for starters. Too many people I don't know, and I don't want to know. Somebody hands me a cold beer. I drink it without further delay. Much better.

The band, Eve of Destruction, has been playing for the last hour or so. I was all set to mock and despise, but in actual fact they are very good. Powerful. Nikola's voice, in particular, has sent my bone marrow a-tremble. Perhaps heavy metal rock is where the real musical talent lies. That, and opera. The rest of the music world could do exactly what they're doing, but without the music. Thing is, you don't get groupies if you're poet, or an actor. Well not in the same way. Even Eve of Destruction has groupies. Of sorts – flock of local sheep sorts. Surprised not to mention shocked not to find Teodora baaing amongst them. But the boys seem to be perfectly happy with their ovine lot. Or just wasted enough to think they are.

Nikola of course sings every song for Elena's ears only. He fixes her with a meaningful gaze, then belts out unintelligible things that seem to impress the crap out of the audience. Apparently, he's singing the

Judas Priest version of 'Diamonds and Rust', except it's in German. Even Elena stops eating cherries and looks up, smiling at him. I think maybe I should like what they have, want it for myself. My man on a stage, singing stuff for my ears only. My own and only man. Something like that.

But I don't. I don't want romance. For that's what this is, a romance. Girls like Elena, they like to play it vague, but what they actually want is tangible. What they want is a solid proof that someone wants them; red roses and stiff cocks. But most of all, I suspect, they want romance.

'So,' I say. 'Have you set a date yet?'

Elena looks alarmed. 'Date for what?'

'For your wedding day.'

'Are you fucking with me?'

I shake my head. 'Course not.'

'Do I look like the marrying kind?'

'Yes?'

'Well I'm not,' she says. 'Not a white wedding type of a girl.'

'Black wedding, then. Are you a black wedding type of a girl?'

'No. Not all girls want to get married, okay. You disappoint me, bugger off.'

Elena turns her back on me and walks away. I thought she wanted me to do the walking. But it doesn't matter any more. For I've just spotted Iva. Sitting on a guy's lap. Who clearly is that old asshole, Vladimir From Osijek.

I'm a bit drunk, so I march over to them no problemo. 'Hello stranger.' Iva doesn't look all too pleased to see me. I make sure I don't show her how sad this makes me, or how pissed off I am with her right now (very on both accounts). Vladimir looks at me in a quasi-scientific sort of way. Like I was a bug under his toy magnifying glass. There's a space on the bench they're sitting on, or rather: half a space. All they need to do is shift a bit to the left. So I can sit down. But they choose not to. 'Hello Iva, how are you?'

Iva blows a runaway hair off her forehead. I know this gesture all too well. And I also know what it means – Iva's trying to buy herself some time. So she can face me. Me, for fuck's sake. 'Oh, you know…'

'No I don't know,' I say. 'I wouldn't have asked if I knew. I tried to find out, but it was like, Iva doesn't live here no more. She's away on business. All hush-hush. And shit.'

'Yeah,' she says. 'I was just about to say it was a busy few months… Before you so rudely interrupted. Some things never change.'

'Busy doing what?'

'Screwing Vladimir… Mostly.'

Vladimir grins like an idiot toucan. As a child, I used to play the Which Chimera? game. I made it up all by my clever self. It's a great game, based on spotting an animal/bird connection in every person you meet. Well according to this game, Vladimir would make a good hyena-toucan chimera. You'd really have to see him to believe it. Except you wouldn't actually want to do no such thing. See Vladimir, that is. It would give you nightmares for life.

'Stupid is what stupid does.' I didn't exactly plan to say this, but I'm so glad I did.

'What?' Vladimir looks at me in a painfully exaggerated disbelief. The affected, abnormally tall cunt. 'Did she say what I think she said?'

I swear Iva then tries to warn me with her eyes. 'What was that, Iva?' I ask. 'Got something stuck in your eye? Can't see proper no more?'

'Go home, Helena,' she says. 'Sleep it off.'

'While you still have a home to go to,' says Vladimir.

I turn to him. 'What the fuck's that supposed to mean, you ridiculous freak?'

He looks about, checking for witnesses no doubt, before saying, 'Have you not heard? A big bad wolf is coming to visit in the night, and he's going to burn your house down, with all your family fast asleep in their beds, you little Serbian whore.'

'Vladimir!' Iva jumps off his lap. 'Shut the fuck up!' She grabs my arm. 'You! Come with me!'

'I hear the Chetnik scum from across the water are closing in on Vukovar,' says Vladimir. 'I bet Helena here is dying to take over the stage, organise a little welcome party.'

I snatch my arm back from Iva's sweaty grip. 'First of all, you sound stupid when you speak. Secondly, and only because I'm curious to find out what goes on in a head of your average gorilla, why do you think I'd want to organise a Chetnik party? And just so you know, you will be burning in eternal flames for making me use those specific words in that specific formation, you moron!'

'Muddying the waters, are we?' Vladimir winks at me. 'Don't even try it, darling, your secret's well and truly out. Iva told me you're an über Serb. Father from Petrova Gora, mother from Knin, can't get any more bloodthirsty than that.'

'Vladimir,' says Iva. 'You're talking about Elena, the one over there… This is Helena!'

'Yeah,' I say. 'Get it right, prick!'

Vladimir places the tips of his fingers on his lower lip. Like he needs to look any more dumb. 'Oh, my! Thousand apologies!'

'Not accepted,' I say. 'And if I tell Elena you mixed the two of us up, she's going to shoot you in the head. So you either give me a thousand deutschmark, or you're dead so-called man.'

'Very funny,' he says.

'Yeah,' says Iva. 'Very funny, now come!' She hustles me past the stage and the square flower patch, and all the way into the vegetable garden. Iva's very strong, physically, as well as emotionally. I used to be scared of her, but would never ever admit it.

'I'm scared of you,' I say. 'You are extremely strong. And scary.'

'That's nice,' she says. 'Helena, listen to me now. Are you listening?'

'I am! Christ! What's so bloody important all of a sudden? Where were you when I had important stuff to tell you? I was really lonely, you cunt!'

And here I start to cry. I can't explain it. I just am, crying like a baby. I even drop to the ground, like my knees have given up. They haven't really, I just don't wish to be too visible in this state, especially as I'm starting to experience a double-strong urge to take off all my clothes. Except there aren't any familiar attic corners for me to run to and hide amongst their slanty angles. Iva kneels next to me, puts her arms around me. 'It's okay, it's fine, it's going to be okay… Relax, for God's sake, you're as stiff as a board.'

I am not sure I'm enjoying this situation. Iva holding me, I mean. It's weird. I wish she would stop, but don't want to appear rude. So I stop snivelling. I get a grip. 'Note to self,' I say. 'Don't drink beer. It makes me go all sentimental.'

But the hug situation with Iva is still going on. I wait for another fifteen seconds, then try to peel away. But she won't let me. Wherever my body goes, hers follows. 'Er,' I say. 'Er.' She then places her head on my chest. What the fuck's Iva's head doing on my chest. I go to remove it, but hesitate. Both my hands are now levitating around ten centimetres above her head, unsure of where to go, what to do next. I just hope my nipples don't randomly pop out. They do that sometimes.

'I've missed you so much,' she mumbles. 'But what else could I've done? You wouldn't take sides, damn you… You had to stay the same.'

Turns out that extreme politics was in. Nationalism was the new black. Everyone knew this by now, except for me. At least that's what Iva tells me. Then she tries to kiss me. I mean, she's already kissed me by then, several times smack on the lips; I thought perhaps this also was the new black I knew nothing about, and so I let her. But the next minute, her tongue is trying to push its way in between my tightly clenched teeth.

Unsure of what else I could do, I blow a raspberry.

Iva immediately loosens her clearly lesbian grip. 'What are you doing?'

'Me?' I feel fully entitled to sound indignant, for a change. 'Me? What are you doing?'

Iva wipes her mouth with a sleeve. Truth to be told, it is me who should be wiping off all trace of her assault. Aggressors are clever like that. Make you feel it's all your fault. I read about it in one of my dad's books on the art of war.

'Sorry,' says Iva. 'I got a little carried away.'

'No shit.'

'Come on, Helena,' she says. 'You must know how I feel about you.'

'All I know is you seemed angry with me, like, all the time,' I say. 'So angry you let that guy almost rape me.'

'How many times do you need me to say I'm sorry?'

'And then you disappeared.'

'Just tell me this,' says Iva. 'Before I did all that bad stuff, do you remember all those times I tried to show you how much I loved you, and you pushed me away?'

I think very hard.

'Anything?' she says. 'Nothing? Not even one?'

'I refuse to say anything that would make me look ignorant.'

'Since when?'

'You're hilarious,' I say. 'For a neo-Nazi.'

'Bullshit.'

'Not!'

'For your information, Neo-Nazis are supremacists,' says Iva. 'And Croats don't wish for supremacy over anyone, we just want to keep what's rightfully ours. But I know you don't give a shit, not really, so what's the point?'

'I do give a shit! About the things that really matter – not politics! Politics, Iva!'

'I don't want to argue, Helena. Not with you.'

I can feel my eyes welling up again. 'Seriously, Iva, why did you have to leave me like that? I do give a shit, I think this really may be the end of the world as we know it, and I hate going it alone. We could've seen it out together, but now it's too late. And the whole thing feels like a punishment, even though I have no idea what I did wrong.'

Iva smiles. She's looking tired now, I notice, and pale. Like all the life's drained away. 'You were supposed to feel it. The way I was with you... You know? The way I was with nobody else but you.'

The way I left it with Iva, was with her warning me to choose a side before a side chooses me. I do not take very kindly to threats of any sort, so I told her to go fuck herself and take her fascist friends with her. 'You make me want to throw up,' I said. And then I threw up right there, in the cabbage patch. That was the last time I saw Iva.

IT'S LIKE THAT

I come round into the slurry pit of somebody else's life. I know this is not my life, couldn't be, I'm not so stupid as to own such a thing. I also know my body's going to hurt, but then again my body always does that. Hurts. Kid you not. You point a finger at it and it's bruised. Anyway. Time to face the music. I unpeel my eyelids. Where am I. Question mark. And when – it's dark in here, but I'm not exactly sure if this is dusk or dawn kind of darkness. Normally, this wouldn't bother me too much, but there are times when a girl could do with having a semblance of her so-called bearings. Like for example, right now.

I check in with my body. Feels like it's all there. Clothes included. Not that I've ever slutted around, but hey, it doesn't take much for a girl to lose her clothing without her exact volition. Moving swiftly on, I make out I'm lying on a couch, wrapped up in a fluffy blanket. Which smells funny, but not entirely unpleasant. Mostly whisky and cigarettes. I try to unknot my thoughts, determine what latest faithful string of events got me here in the first place. Or should this read the last. Well no wonder I never managed to win anything in my entire so-called life.

Ought to write a book about this one day, titled The Ultimate Loser's Guide to Winning. Or The Ultimate Winner's Guide to Losing. Work in progress.

Seriously though.

Where am I.

'It's definitely going down, then.'

Huston, we have company. How about that for a game changer.

'Looks like it, brother... Should've run when we still had a chance.'

Two voices. Male. Why couldn't there be a couple of nice ladies, sharing a pot of camomile tea. For a change. I squint into the darkness, make out a soft silhouette, then another. Oh yeah: I was at Nikola and Elena's leaving do, wasn't I.

My nose is itchy.

'There's nowhere to run.' Male One's voice sounds thin, like its owner's about to cry. A grown man, crying, how very embarrassing for him. 'Or hide. Not any more.'

'Australia. Germany.' Male Two is softer. Nicer. Familiar, even. I hope he wins. 'Or Argentina – they took in plenty of Croatian war criminals after the Second World War.'

Male One laughs. 'Fuck off back to Mother Serbia, will you?'

'No can do. Vukovar born and bred, see.'

'In that case, let's just have another drink.' Male One gets up. I shrink as far back into the sofa as I can. But he only strolls over to the bookshelf, pulls out a bottle, then returns to his spot. There are no books on that shelf, I notice. Only bottles, and a pile of records.

Not a bad idea for a simple life. I'm going to copy it when I get home. Male One unscrews the top and throws it out of the window. 'Now we have no choice but to finish the bottle.'

'Something to do.' Male Two lights up, takes a drag. I close my eyes quick, so he doesn't notice I'm watching him. Make yourself invisible, Helena. Go on, you can do it, if you really truly wanted to. 'I could've run to London. Paris, maybe. Or straight for America, leave this tired old European Weltschmerz crap behind for once and for all.'

Did someone just say Weltschmerz.

'The world doesn't want conscientious objectors,' says Male One. 'It wants war criminals. Guess if we committed a couple of heinous war crimes–'

'And pulled off at least one genocide–'

'We'd stand a chance of becoming Citizens of the World.'

'Is that what they call it these days?'

Both men laugh. At what, I'm not too sure.

'Well, brother,' says Male Two. 'Looks like we'll just have to stay here and fight.'

'No other choice.'

'None whatsoever.'

They drink in silence for a while. I feel sad. Just like that, out of the blue, I'm officially feeling sad, and lonely (and, I got to say it, blue). Plus my nose is still itching. Fucking fluff. Iva must've left me here, even though she knows I'm sensitive to fluff and feathers and many other things, potentially. Trust her, and her misguided gay-love to wrap me up like a mummy, leave me behind with a couple of raping soldier wannabes. Yeah, I remember now. Admittedly it's a bit slo-mo, nothing's real, strawberry fields forever, but it is still a memory.

'Would you shoot me?' asks Male One.

'How can you even ask me such a question?'

'Get real, Petar...' Petar? I know a Petar. 'Push comes to shove?'

'Never!'

'You'd have to shoot me, you wouldn't have a choice.'

'Don't tell me what I'd do!'

'Look, you immovable Serbian object, all I'm saying is, you'd have to shoot me – or get shot.'

'Okay, Ante, I get your point,' says Petar. 'Trust a Croat to point the obvious.'

'Trust a Croat?'

'Yeah – trust you planning to turn on a brother while you're still breaking bread with him.'

Whoops a daisy. There will be tears before bedtime, as Dad used to say, and he was right. But only because Teodora insisted on doing annoying stuff, like talking and breathing, and sooner or later I couldn't help slapping her.

'Fuck you, brother,' says Ante. 'And fuck your Serbian code of honour.'

'Too right there's honour.'

'Yeah,' says Ante. 'Honour amongst thieves.'

They start laughing again. I don't get this nationalistic doubletalk. The ins and outs of it. What goes and what doesn't. I don't get these people, this land, this town. Maybe that's because there isn't anything to get.

'I hear the Yugoslav People's Army, what's left of it, is fast approaching,' says Ante. 'Proper Chetniks, born and bred in Serbia, none of your I'm a Croatian Serb and proud of it bullshit. These guys mean business, and they are coming here to claim what never belonged to them in the first place. They are joined by the mercenary mother fuckers, paid soldiers, scum of the earth... I hear they've already made camps south of Vukovar. Roasting the pigs and oxen they took from our peasants, drinking their wine, raping their wives and daughters, same old, same old.'

There's silence. One of the men clears his throat. More silence. I feel sleepy.

Ante continues, 'I was wondering if you had any more details.'

'You mean, because I'm a Serb?'

'Yes, Petar, because you're a Serb.'

'Straight answer? From a Croat? Well, now I've seen it all.' Petar pauses for a moment. 'Listen, Ante... I've known you all my life. We grew up together, you've always been my best friend, and nothing's gonna change that. I don't want this war. I don't want to fight anyone. All I want is to listen to my music, ride my bike around this rotten apple called Europe, and to get this strange girl to like me.'

What strange girl.

'I know,' says Ante. 'I feel you, brother. But the bastards won't let us.'

He's starting to sound a bit snivelly. What did I say about those tears. All I need now is a bedtime, their bedtime, so I can get out of here. All this war talk, it's making me feel nervous. With my mind's eye, and thanks to Ante, I can clearly see the dense rows of Chetniks marching in, black beards caterwauling across the Slavonian plain, heavy boots crashing through the wheat and corn fields, ghostly shapes funnelling through the forests, advancing towards Vukovar with a murderous intent.

Brrr. It's getting cold around here. Must be the new dawn rising.

I look under the sheets. Petar's head is burrowing in between my legs, positively in a nice way. He looks up, smiles at me. I laugh. I feel happy now.

It takes him a while, but when he does eventually resurface, I want to ask him to go back down there and continue the noble work of pleasuring me, the work he was so clearly born to do. Sluttery must run in our family, after all. Teodora is a bona fide nympho incapable of keeping her knickers on, Mummy Dearest is pregnant again, and at the ripe old age of very old, and now look at me, can't seem to get enough of this thing called sex. 'For the record: you were the strange girl I was talking about. The strange girl I wanted to like me.'

'Betty Blue strange?'

'Huh?' says Petar.

'Béatrice Dalle in Betty Blue strange?' I say. 'Or Catherine Deneuve in Repulsion strange?'

'You choose.' He leans over and kisses me on the lips. More kisses. More lips. More Petar. 'I'm good with Helena strange.'

I sit up. 'I would've preferred it if you picked Béatrice Dalle.'

'Why?' Petar tries to pull me on top of him, but I pretend to resist.

'Because she's cool,' I say. 'Even her so-called madness is cool.'

'Okay.' He throws his hands up in the air, stretches long and dare I say, hard. 'And the other one?'

'You mean Catherine Deneuve?'

'Is she the repulsive one?'

'Could it be...' I trace my finger along that most deliciously smooth alleyway that leads from his elbow to his armpit. Believe the technical term for this part of man's anatomy must be something like the inner upper arm. Never did find biology all that interesting. Applied biology, however, is a completely different matter. 'That you have no idea who I'm talking about?'

'I've told you, baby,' he says. 'Bikes and records. I'm that simple.'

'Practically Zen.'

'What she said. Now come here.'

Well I've never heard of a Zen master who was also a wizard in bed.

As I had discovered earlier at Nikola's house, you can only keep the lid on a fluff-induced sneeze for a definite period of time.

'Achoo!' My cover thus blown to pieces, all I could think of doing was run for another. And so I did, I jumped off the sofa, made for the closest exit point, i.e. the door, opened it with far too much force and bang straight into my face, ending up knocking myself slightly unconscious. Luckily, it turned out

Ante and Petar weren't at all intent on raping me. Instead, they did all they could to help me regain my lost bearings, stop the nosebleed and hold a bag of ice on the dent-lump chimera that formed smack in the middle of my forehead.

As it turned out, Petar was my Peter. Or at least the Petar I wanted to make mine, by way of cleverly seducing him, somehow.

'So you're a pacifist-Serb,' I said. 'Bit of an oxymoron, won't you agree?'

'Why?' he asked. 'Do you have a problem with that?'

'Just checking.'

'Bullshit.' He passed me a cigarette, said, 'Why are you being like this?'

'Like what?'

He shrugged. 'All weird and jumpy. Lurking in corners, scaring people half to death.'

'Me, scaring people?' I wanted to laugh, but my head felt far too fragile for such a dynamic activity. 'Me?'

'Yes, you. Unpredictable. And far too fickle.' Petar touches the tip of my nose. 'And your nose is too big.'

I watched Ante crawl onto the sofa and dive under my fluffy cover. The next second he was snoring. I don't envy many people. But right then, I envied Ante almost as much as I envied a typical American college cheerleader crying over a broken nail.

Petar insisted on taking me home. As he pushed his bike out from Nikola's yard, a car pulled up on the front lawn. The driver wore fatigues with Croatian

Garda markings. I had seen Garda members around before, but never this up close and personal. Nor had I ever looked at them with this much anxiety. The guy got out in a hurry, then did a full body-shake, like dogs do after they get out of the Danube.

'That's better,' he said. 'Way better!'

I tug on the back of Petar's trousers, as he's wearing a vest so no sleeves to tug on, whisper, 'Pretend you didn't see him!'

Petar puts his free arm around my shoulders. 'Everything alright?'

'Everything's sweet,' said the man. 'Except I almost didn't make the run.'

'Oh yeah?' said Petar. 'Bummer.'

'I took Nikola and his bird to the train station in Vinkovci – I was their getaway driver.' The man said. 'But we hit three checkpoints before Nuštar, three checkpoints. Thorough. We almost missed the train. Our boys, dead thorough.'

'Good job,' said Petar. 'All around.'

'Yeah.' The man punches the air a few times, then kicks an innocent bystander cherry tree for no apparent reason. 'Phow–phow! Of course, Nikola will have to come back. I told him his trip was a waste of time, because he'll only have to come back, like, straight away.'

I poke my head from underneath Petar's wing. 'Why?'

The man points at the Garda badge on his uniform. 'The Croatian government is recruiting. Every able body. That's what they said. Everybody. Men and women of fighting age. But mostly men.' He nods at

Petar. 'I expect you'll be joining soon, what choice do we have, eh, we have no choice but to protect what's ours.'

He was obviously thinking that Petar was a Croat. Just like I suspected all along, these guys couldn't tell the difference between a Serb and a Croat if their lives depended on it. Which they kind of do. It has come to that.

Petar revved up the engine, patted the seat behind him. 'Hop on, girl!' I did as I was told, and I held on tight. The Gardist saluted us off. What a dickhead.

There was a red Saab parked up in our drive. Little too early for guests I would've hoped. So here's to hoping. Petar manoeuvred the bike across the narrow strip of grass between the driveway and the flower bed, and parked up in front of the gates.

'Ask me in.'

'May as well, looks like we have an open house.'

'Helena.'

His voice sounded serious, his face looked it. I wished I knew what that meant. To be completely honest, I could never read people, I only pretended that I could. It's a shocker, I know. 'What?'

'Ask me nicely. Like you mean it.'

'Please, Petar, come on in and fuck me senseless,' I said. 'Is this nice enough for you?'

He gave me another mysterious look, put his helmet back on, then turned to leave.

Crap. I didn't want him to leave, and leave me here all alone. 'Petar!' He didn't stop. I had to run after him, grab his arm. 'Stay. Please stay.' I had never done anything like this before, I have never begged anyone to stay. Well I guess he'll now just have to marry me or something.

We walked to the house, hand in hand. Up the stairs, onto the veranda and then I had to stop. Couldn't, wouldn't go any further. 'Let's go back.'

'Back?' said Petar. 'Back where?'

That very moment, Dad appeared, carrying a couple of suitcases. The red one, and the soft blue leather one I always bagsied for our summer holiday. Teodora was too slow. Too damn slow for me.

'Helena! Great timing!' He dropped the luggage and gave me a hug that confirmed my fear that something wasn't right here. 'Grab your ten favourite possessions, you have five minutes, and counting! And who's this strapping young lad? Hello, I'm Helena's father, do you think you could give me a hand?'

'Sure,' said Petar. 'My name's Petar, how do you do.'

They shake hands. Exchange grave looks. Give me a break. Petar grabs the suitcases. 'Where to?'

'The car's outside… The boot should be open,' said Dad. Petar nodded like a good boy, marched off. How did he do this, my father. How did he always manage to get people to do stuff for him. Suddenly, I feel annoyed. Mostly with Dad. My old man. This random old man who got to be my father, and never knew what to do about it. 'Helena! I thought I told you to get a move on!'

'No!'

'Right, young lady, you now have three minutes left to get five of your favourite possessions!' He was glaring at me like I never seen him glare at anyone or anything before. I always suspected he was a murdering spy. 'I don't have time for this! Get on with it, go!'

'Are you deaf?' I screamed. 'I'm not going anywhere!'

'For fuck's sake, girl!' My dad rarely raised his voice, but when he did, he kind of meant it. And you were supposed to know that he meant it. Well: yawn and zzzzz and I don't think so. He went on, 'I had enough of your selfish attitude, and your spoilt brat act, and most of all, I had enough of your forever feeling sorry for yourself. What's so bloody wrong with your life? Hey, princess? Where's the fucking pea?' He ran his fingers through his hair. 'I'm your father! So you'll do as I ask! You hear me? Go get your stuff, and don't make me repeat myself!'

Just then, my mum and sister appeared on the veranda, all dressed up and ready to roll. Dressed for their role. But what's the play. The stage's all set up, the actors seem keen; the whole thing seems to be in full swing, but where's my script. It's probably a shitty script, anyway, but still. It would've been nice to be included. There was a burning hole in the middle of my chest. My body started to shake. I had to get away, find my own corner of the world to hide in. I had to get to safety. A man hopped onto the stage. I knew him. Dad's boss. Branko. He was there when I was told my godfather Dragan was murdered. I liked Branko. Perhaps he could be my new godfather.

Mum rushed over, gave me a hug that was

identical to the one previously served on me by my father. 'Thank God you're here! Grab a few things, darling, be quick! We're getting out of Vukovar, there's no time to waste!'

I glanced over Mum's shoulder at Teodora. She was just standing there, clutching a bag full of her worthless crap, her face soaked with crocodile tears of epic proportions. She's got to be the saddest one, doesn't she. Well she can keep that role to be sure.

'I'm not going,' I said. 'Leave me alone.'

'Don't speak to your mother like that!' Dad beelined towards me. I covered my eyes with my hands, and waited. He has never hit me before. I wondered what would it feel like, to be hit by your own father.

'Stefan!' Mum cried. 'No!'

There was a sound of struggle that could've lasted for a few moments, or a few lifetimes.

'Enough!' I heard Branko saying. 'Relax, man, just breathe!'

'What's going on?' Petar! I opened my eyes, letting in a little of what was going on around me, and found him standing right in front of me, removing my hands from my face. I wanted everyone else in the world to cease to exist. Except Petar and me. Helena & Petar's Super Safe Sanctuary. Catchy. 'You okay?'

'My dad wants me to leave Vukovar. I don't want to go. I want go to my bedroom. Please help me get to my bedroom.'

'Petar, is it?' Dad sort of strolled over, smoothing down his linen jacket, making himself look presentable again, and totally in control. I took a step back anyway. 'Don't worry, Helena, I'm fine. Really.

I'm over it. I'm sorry I lost my temper. But listen, this is hardly the time to be a rebel. Petar, tell her, please… I don't know how well you know my daughter, but she seems to trust you… Maybe you can tell her that this is not the time to be stubborn. Or different. Maybe she'll listen to you. Because she sure as hell isn't listening to me. God knows why.'

For the record, it's not my fault I'm different. It's my parents' fault, it the genes they handed me down. I considered telling them that right there and then, but decided to wait for a less hectic moment. Only so they could hear me better.

'Come on, darling,' said Dad. 'We talked about this. Get in the car. It'll be an adventure, you'll see.'

'Helena?' Petar smiled at me. 'Your father is asking you to get into the car with your mum and your sister, okay? You need to get out, Vukovar is no longer safe.'

'Petar can come along,' said Dad. 'Petar? Would you like to come with us?'

Petar shakes his head. 'Helena?'

'I can't leave.' I almost bit my tongue in two, my teeth were chattering so bad.

'What did she say?' Teodora, who else. 'Let's just go without her, Daddy.

If she loves it here so much.'

'Shut up, you,' said Mum. 'I wouldn't go either, if I wasn't pregnant!'

'That was hardly helpful,' said Dad. 'Matija, would you mind terribly waiting in the car?'

Mum picked up her bags and left without uttering another word. Teodora ran after her, like a spastic puppy. That was the last time I saw them.

I FEEL LOVE

So here we are now, Petar and me, lying naked in my bed, teasing each other's brain with musical riddles, teasing each other's body with all that we have left after being at it for the last twelve hours straight. My father, my dad, my old man, that bloody man I still feel so angry with, and will continue to feel that way for the rest of my life no doubt, had finally agreed to leave me be, on condition that Petar brings me over to Vukovar hospital by 6pm that evening. Apparently, there was this German doctor who popped over to organise safe convoys out of town, for hospital patients and such like. Why a German doctor would want to hang around the crusty old clientele of Vukovar hospital I'll never understand, but Dad insisted I go find him, so eventually I said yeah, right, whatever.

'Promise me,' said Dad. 'Promise you'll find Dr Miller and leave Vukovar tonight. It has got to be tonight, because this place will be swamped by the Chetniks by tomorrow morning. Petar? Promise me you'll make sure she's there tonight. No later than 6pm.'

'I solemnly promise,' I said. 'I do. Please don't give yourself a stroke. Bon voyage, Daddy.'

To make the already most awkward situation even more awkward, this was where my dad started to cry. Never saw him cry before, wish he kept it that way. He hugged me again, and I didn't want his hug. I didn't want his tears on my shoulder. Or my err conscience. So I pulled away. He stood there, all by lonesome, for like a moment or two; embarrassing. Thank fuck Petar was there. He stepped right up, and offered his hand. Men are a little bit like dogs, I reckon, because Dad put up his hand without even thinking about it, without even thinking to himself, "Shit, son, can't you see I'm a little busy here with saying good bye to my unruly godawful daughter who won't listen to a word I say and whom I may well never see again ever in my life on account of her, or me, or maybe even both of us dying somewhere along the way in this fucking shithole of a town in this fucking shithole of this so-called life, fuck me I can see clearly now that we never had a chance and now you want WHAT, you want to shake my fucking hand, you fucking moron, you."

'Rest assured, Mr Ferlan,' said Petar. 'I shall accompany your daughter on her way to Vukovar hospital and make sure she's on that convoy out of town by tonight.'

Like I was a:

a) child;

b) slave girl, or

c) sack of potatoes.

Anyway, they shook on it, and I didn't any visible fuss because I wanted Dad to leave already. So I could finally sleep with Petar. Which was exactly what happened next.

I ran upstairs as fast as I could, and not only because I'm a common tart. No: for some bizarre reason, I wanted to steal one last glance at my dad, before he drove away. I clambered on the sofa and pushed open the roof window. There he still was, one hand on the car door, another laid across his chest. He took off his glasses, cleaned them with one of his dotty handkerchiefs, then carefully placed them back on top of his nose. He looked long and hard towards the house. He may have been surveying his kingdom, as far as I could tell. Which would've been a silly thing to do. A waste of time. Why fret. Go have your holiday in peace. Enjoy. Disappear. Go. Run, rabbit, run.

It had taken a little persuasion, but in the end Petar agreed with me that there was hardly any real need to go down to the hospital. I mean, the chances of some German doctor being stupid enough to be pulling people out of Vukovar just because a couple of soldier-wannabes decided to start playing war in the woods around Vukovar were as slim as my chances of, err, breaking my nail whilst cheerleading an American college football team. We decided we'd have a little rest, instead, then get out of Vukovar first thing tomorrow morning. On Petar's bike. In total style. Hurrah to the spirit of adventure, double hurrah to having guts to follow it. Petar said that most people guarding the barricades were local boys, Vukovar born and inbred. Also known as: Croatian Garda. Or: Croatian Garda my ass. In any case, Petar knew them all. The plan was that he was going to tell them he's my taxi driver, dropping me off at Vinkovci train station, then returning to join their so-called ranks. Which of course wouldn't be the case. Once we're out, we'd stay out. Together. As plans go, this one didn't bore me titless. So I knew it was a brilliant one.

We are watching Down by Law on my video player. The tape's long overdue back at the videotheque, but the owners seem to have fled town so I got to keep it. Yey. Petar's laughing at Roberto explaining to his cellmates Jack and Zach how come he's ended up in jail. He wants me to rewind the scene. Again. I'm sort of pleased. Or at least not annoyed by Petar's demands – now that's what I call a relationship progress. We're lying on my bed, as close to one another as our bodies would allow before starting to merge. His hand's on my naked thigh. He squeezes it a bit every time he laughs. Good old Roberto. Play it again, will you *ragazzo*.

We're walking around the vegetable garden, picking and eating late strawberries, all warm and juicy from the sun. Petar picks a gooseberry, pops it into his mouth, then spits it out.

'What the fuck was that?' he asks. 'So sour.'

Aww. His first gooseberry. Something to remember me by, besides being the hottest lay he's ever likely to have.

'Do you like pasta? Great,' I say. 'So we need a few tomatoes, and… Can you pick some basil?'

'Basil?'

'Over there… See? In the herb garden behind you.'

He returns triumphant, carrying a large bunch of parsley. I laugh and I laugh, like this is the funniest thing that has ever happened to me in my whole entire life.

We're sitting on the outside sofa, eating sticky watermelon triangles, having a pip spitting contest. Miko walks by, takes one look at Petar, then jumps straight onto his lap. Just like that. Purring like mad, he's looking at Petar with so much devotion I'm feeling not only flabbergasted but also a little jealous. And greatly pleased at the same time. With myself, with Miko, and especially with Petar. I have never been this happy around another person before. In actual fact, I don't believe I have ever felt happy before he came along, full stop.

Back in my bedroom, I'm singing into my hairbrush. 'Here Comes Your Man'. The Pixies. Petar's watching me. I am singing at the top of my voice, not holding anything back. Miko's tail starts flicking about. That philistine cat.

I've lit at least ten candles, before losing count. It's dark now. Wonder where my dad is. Wonder if they got out of town alright. Petar puts his arms around me, pulls me down onto the bed.

We're dancing to Donna Summer. 'I Feel Love'. I won the LP by coming last at yet another chess tournament I made myself participate in. Dad's an International Master, so I thought I'd impress him by entering and winning lots of shiny trophies to add to his, correction: to our collection. It was a clean, simple plan, which didn't quite work out on account of my being crap at chess. Even Teodora was better at it than me, that's how crap I was. And still am.

I ceased trying to impress anyone a long time ago, which is a relief and all round improvement to be sure. Then again, one of the consolation prizes I was given was Parallel Lines by Blondie, a crazy thing to give a nine-year-old chess loser girl. I guess trying to impress random people and failing miserably has its advantages after all.

I'm dreaming about a witch chasing me. She's all dressed up in black, and every time I dare turn around, I see the darkness in her eyes has spread further and deeper and blacker than before. I run to Baba Lepa's house. The gate's open wide. I enter into the front yard, find myself surrounded by a herd of wild horses. I know they're untamed, even though all they're doing is standing around, looking depressed, their heads hanging loose, their once magnificent glossy manes lowered all the way down to the dusty ground. I clap my hands, shout at them to wake up, to get a grip, to run free whilst they still can. The witch catches up with me. I throw my arms around a horse's neck, whisper, 'Save me, save me, please save me so I can save you back.' But the horse just stands there, lifeless. The darkness swallows us up.

I'm in bed, crying. Petar has his arms firmly around me, and won't let me run for my corner. Won't let me run.

233

'There, there,' he keeps saying. As if I was his baby. 'I'm right here. It's all good.'

There's a sound of distant thunder. The storm is on its way.

I look into the drinks cabinet. I'm not usually allowed to come anywhere near it, but whilst the cat's away and all that. My parents have a vast and intriguing collection of booze. I congratulate them on this in my thoughts. But I'm not after interesting. I'm after getting high and forgetting the low. I get half-way up the stairs when I realise that drinking whisky always sends me deranged, and not in a good way. I usually ignore these sudden insights, but this time I decide to listen. I turn back and swap the bottle of bourbon, the only souvenir my dad brought back from his trip to New York, for a bottle of vodka. By the time I return to bed, Petar's fast asleep. I feel lonely. So I wake him up.

A clasp of thunder roars outside my window. I get up with a jolt, my heart pounding like crazy. I look outside. The world's on fire. I go back to bed. 'Petar. Petar. Hey. Petar.'

He stirs. 'Hey, honey… What's up?'

'The world's on fire. Think we may have been struck by lightning.'

Petar watches the pretty lights dancing around the room. 'Shit!' He jumps out of the bed.

'Where are you going?' I ask. 'Come back, it's still night time.'

'Get up, Helena! Get up!' He pulls on his jeans,

throws over the dress I wore to death yesterday. 'We've got to get out of here. Now!'

'You're scaring me!' I don't feel too well. The vodka has given me a headache. It always does. 'It's just a storm. Lightning struck some old tree–'

'No!' Petar grabs my arms, and basically lifts me to my feet. 'It's started. Fuck! We left it too late!'

'What? It's not late, we have plenty of time… It's only a storm.'

'Dress! On!' He helps me pull the dress over my head. 'I need you to do exactly as I say, okay?'

'But I'm not wearing any knickers.'

'Don't worry about the knickers,' he says. 'The bag!'

Petar had made me put together a bag for our morning trip. A passport, money, a few pairs of underwear, that sort of thing. Silly things. I only did to keep him happy. 'But–'

'No buts!' Petar drags me down the stairs, and onto the veranda.

I'm about to complain about the unnecessarily rough treatment, but the sight in front of my eyes makes me instantly forget all my prior so-called grievances.

Because it is hell out there. Everything's on fire, caught up in bright-red and orange flames, enveloped in thick curls of acrid black smoke.

'Stay low!' Petar shouts. 'Don't let go of my hand!'

'Never!'

He squeezes tight. 'We're going to get the bike, okay?'

I nod, keep nodding. Just then, a quince tree to the

left of us spontaneously combusts. Peter covers me with his body, shouts, 'Stay here!'

'No!'

'Stay! I'll get the bike!'

'No, Petar!' I cling to him, he breaks free. 'No!'

'I'll be right back!' He kisses my hair. 'I promise. I love you.'

I look on, as Petar disappears into the world of darkness and smoke. This was the last time I saw him.

I wait for what seems like forever. There's no sign of Petar. Slowly but surely the light infringes upon the dying inferno. I should search for Petar, but I don't want to. What I want is more vodka. And a few painkillers. And to sleep. I get to my feet, steadying myself against wooden railings. 'Miko!' My voice won't come out. There's nothing. No voice. 'Miko?' Nothing.

The next moment, a deafening sound reverberates through every bone in my body. The ground starts to shake. "First the worst storm ever," I think. "Now the earthquake. I know what this is, it's the end of the world." There's a hissing noise, coming closer fast. It explodes inside my head. Everything turns silent.

I come round into the slurry pit of somebody else's life. I know this is not my life, couldn't be my life, I'm not so stupid as to own such a thing. I open my eyes, first my right, then left. I've been here before. As thoughts go, this one is as reassuring as can be. Under the circumstances. And as concrete as it gets. Because, I don't know where I am. I don't know what time it is. Or day. Most pressingly, though, I don't know how safe it is. All I know is that my name's Helena Ferlan, I am not in my bedroom, and I need God to help me get the fuck out of here, like, now.

A shiny black boot appears at my eye level. Then another.

'Looks like we've got ourselves a live one,' a voice says. 'What do you reckon we should do with it?'

THE END

Made in the USA
Columbia, SC
05 January 2018